He wondered what it would take to make Amy Morgan laugh.

Then again, he'd barely been able to tease a smile out of her, and they'd been together most of the day.

Stopping by her office, he knocked on the frame of the open door. "Everything's put away. I'll be back Monday with those extra pieces we talked about." He waved and began backing away. When she called out his name, he paused in the hallway. "Yeah?"

"Things were so hectic today that we never settled on your hourly rate."

"I thought we agreed on zero."

Narrowing her eyes, she tilted her head in a skeptical pose. "Where I'm from, strangers don't do things for free."

"Huh," he said with his brightest grin. "And here I thought we were friends."

While he watched, the brittle cynicism fell away, and the corner of her mouth lifted in a wry grin. "I should warn you—I'm not the easiest person to be friends with."

"That's cool. I like a challenge."

Books by Mia Ross

Love Inspired

MIA ROSS

loves great stories. She enjoys reading about fascinating people, long-ago times and exotic places. But only for a little while, because her reality is pretty sweet. Married to her college sweetheart, she's the proud mom of two amazing kids, whose schedules keep her hopping. Busy as she is, she can't imagine trading her life for anyone else's—and she has a pretty good imagination. You can visit her online at www.miaross.com.

Sugar Plum Season

Mia Ross

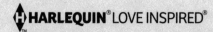

Recycling programs for this product may not exist in your area.

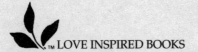 LOVE INSPIRED BOOKS

ISBN-13: 978-0-373-87930-4

Sugar Plum Season

www.Harlequin.com

Printed in U.S.A.

There is no fear in love,
but perfect love casts out fear.
—*1 John* 4:18

For Grandma and Grandpa

Acknowledgments

To the very talented folks who help me
make my books everything they can be:
Elaine Spencer, Melissa Endlich
and the dedicated staff at Love Inspired.

More thanks to the gang at Seekerville
(www.seekerville.net). It's a great place
to hang out with readers—and writers!

I've been blessed with a wonderful network
of supportive, encouraging family and friends.
You inspire me every day!

Chapter One

Carpenter Needed.

Standing outside Arabesque, Amy Morgan studied the sign from the sidewalk in front of her dance studio, wondering if she should've added some details. Unfortunately, she admitted with a sigh, she really didn't have any. She'd spent most of her life at the front of the stage, so she was well versed in choreography, costumes and toe shoes. The more practical elements of set design and construction, not so much. Now that her performing days were behind her, she'd have to learn the mundane aspects of the business, she supposed. She wasn't exactly looking forward to it.

"So, you're looking for a carpenter?"

Startled by the deep voice that came from behind—and far above—her, she spun into a wall of plaid flannel. Looking up, she saw that it led to windblown brown hair, tanned features and a pair of hazel eyes shot through with gold. When their owner smiled, they sparkled with honest male admiration, and her polite response flew straight out of her head.

Once she regained some of her usual composure, she

carefully straightened to her full height, which was still a foot shorter than his. "Yes, I am."

The smile warmed, and he offered her the biggest hand she'd ever seen. Covered in scars, some old and others more recent, it clasped hers with a surprisingly gentle touch. "Jason Barrett. My day job's building custom pieces out at the sawmill, if you'd like some references for my work."

"Amy Morgan." When she registered his name more clearly, she asked, "Are you related to the Barretts who founded the town and run Barrett's Mill Furniture?"

"Yeah, I am." He pointed across the street to the trolley facade of the town's famous diner. "I made the new planter benches for the Whistlestop and replaced the park benches and seats around the old gazebo in the square."

Amy had admired the handmade pieces many times and was impressed with his obvious skill. "They're very nice. You did them by yourself?"

"Start to finish." Cocking his head, he grinned. "I take it that means you're looking for someone who's good at working alone."

"And quickly," she clarified with a sigh. "My uncle Fred was building sets for our production of *The Nutcracker,* but he hurt his back during our family football game on Thanksgiving Day. I've only got three weeks until the show, so I need someone who can pick up where he left off and get everything done in time."

"Sounds doable. Mind if I check things out before I promise something I can't deliver?"

Unlike my ex-fiancé, she grumbled silently. He'd promised her the moon and then bolted when she needed him most. Still, her schoolgirl reaction to this towering stranger bothered her. The last time she'd followed her foolish heart, it hadn't ended well. Who was she kidding? she chided herself. It turned out to be a complete disaster, and she still wasn't over it. But she was a dancer, not a contractor, which meant she needed someone's help. If she waited even a day or two longer to give other people time to respond, there was a good chance the charming sets she'd planned would have to be trimmed back to something less elaborate that could be completed in time.

Being a perfectionist by nature, that simply wasn't acceptable to her. "Sure. Come on in."

"This is real nice, by the way," he said, motioning toward the huge display window. It was decked out with a rendering of Tchaikovsky's famous ballet in miniature, and she'd just finished framing the scene with twinkle lights. "Makes me wanna come see the show."

"I hope lots of people feel the same," she confided. "The studio hasn't been doing all that well in this economy, so Aunt Helen turned it over to me, hoping some new ideas will bring in more business. I'm doing everything I can to make sure she doesn't regret it."

Pulling open the entry door for her, he said, "Helen gave classes here when I was a kid. My mom used to drag my four brothers and me here to get us some culture to go along with the hunting and fishing we did with my dad."

The way he phrased it made her laugh. "Did it work?"

Spreading his arms out, he looked down at his clothes and battered work boots, then grinned at her. "Whattaya think?"

"I don't know," she hedged, tapping her chin while

pretending to study him carefully. "Looks can be deceiving."

"Not with me," he assured her in his mellow Virginia drawl. "What you see is what you get."

How refreshing, she thought as she led him into the studio. In her world, you never knew what was truly going on behind the performer's mask. Here in Barrett's Mill, it was a relief to find people who were content being who they were, rather than acting like something else altogether. Knowing that didn't totally make up for the glittering life she'd left behind, but it helped ease some of the sting that had a way of sneaking up on her when she wasn't prepared for it.

Putting past regrets aside, she surveyed her studio with a sense of pride for what she'd accomplished since Aunt Helen handed over the reins to her. After plenty of scrubbing, painting and refinishing, the original plaster walls and wide-plank floors had a fresh, timeless quality to them. The wide-open space was dominated by the stage, bracketed by faded burgundy velvet curtains she'd replace as soon as she had the money. Structurally, the platform was as sound as the days when she'd starred in her aunt's dance recitals.

So long ago, she thought wistfully. If she'd known her ballet career would end before she was twenty-five, she'd have valued those productions more.

"This music is nice," her visitor commented in a courteous tone that made it clear he'd rather be listening to something else. "What is it?"

"One of Mozart's violin concertos. Number four, I think."

"Pretty," he went on with a grin. "It suits you."

She wasn't sure how to respond to that, so she didn't

say anything. As they made their way to the stage, she found herself appreciating the self-assured nature of Jason's long strides. He was well over six feet tall, with wide shoulders and a powerful build to go with the outdoorsy history he'd mentioned earlier. He had a strong, solid look to him; it made her think of an oak tree that could stand up against any storm nature chose to throw at it. And yet he moved with a confident grace she envied. She'd give anything to walk that freely again.

When he stopped to look at the framed pictures displayed on the wall at stage left, she knew what had drawn his attention and braced herself for the inevitable question. He turned to her with an amazed expression. "This is you?"

"They're all me," she replied politely, the way she always did when someone asked. "Back in my performing days." Sometimes, they struck her as being from another lifetime. Other days, she felt as if she'd just stepped off the stage after taking her bows. When she allowed herself to think about them, she missed those days with an intensity that made her wonder if teaching was really the right decision for her. The problem was, dance was all she'd ever known, which didn't leave her with any other options. She'd simply have to find a way to make the best of things.

"I'm not an artsy kinda guy, but these are incredible. What's this move called?"

Going to join him, she saw where he was pointing and did her best to smile. "An arabesque jump. It was my favorite to perform, so I renamed the studio Arabesque."

His eyes roamed over the rest of the grouping and stopped on one of her dancing Clara in a youth production of the holiday ballet she'd chosen for this year. The photographer had caught her in midair, making her look as if she was flying. It was by far her favorite shot and the one she would have most liked to shred into a million pieces.

Staring at it for a few moments, he looked down at her with a remarkably gentle smile. It was as if he'd sensed her reaction and was making an attempt to ease her discomfort. "Incredible. How old were you?"

"Twelve. I'd been taking classes at a ballet school in D.C. for four years, and that was my first Christmas production."

"Not really," he teased, tapping his finger on a framed print of her as a six-year-old Rosebud. "I was here for this one, and I remember you."

"You do not," she huffed. "I barely remember it myself."

"You came onstage after the other flowers," he corrected her with a grin. "The older ones all stayed in line, doing their thing, while you floated around like a butterfly. They were good dancers, but there was something different about you. Not to mention, I thought you looked like the pretty ballerina in my cousin's jewelry box."

Amy felt a blush creeping over her cheeks, and she blinked up at him in total bewilderment. She'd always assumed boys that age were more interested in bugs and snakes than classical dance, and that he still remembered her all these years later was astounding.

Realizing she'd been staring up at him like a brainless twit in some old-time romance movie, she gave herself a mental shake. "I'm flattered."

A slow, maddening grin stretched across his features,

transforming them into something she was certain most women couldn't resist. Fortunately for her, she'd been burned by a master, and she'd learned to be very cautious around the male species. Since you couldn't accurately predict when they might turn on you, she'd learned it was best to avoid close contact with them whenever possible.

"So, let's see what Fred left you with."

Jason easily leaped onto the low stage, then reached back to offer her a hand up. More than a little jealous of his athletic maneuver, she shook her head. "I'll just take the stairs."

That was all she said, but compassion flooded his eyes, and he jumped down as easily as he'd gone up. "You're hurt, aren't you? That's why you came back here, because something happened and you can't dance anymore."

His quick assessment came in a sympathetic tone that made her want to scream in frustration and weep at the same time. Getting a firm grip on the emotions he'd unleashed, she straightened her back as far as it would go and gazed defiantly up at him. She might have lost a lot of things, but she still had her pride.

"I've changed my mind about the sets," she said curtly. "Thank you for coming in."

He didn't even flinch. Small as she was, most people backed off when she glared at them the way she was doing now. Apparently, Jason was made of sterner stuff, and she grudgingly admitted he had some grit to go with those rugged looks and killer smile. "You're not getting rid o' me that easy, Miss Amy Morgan."

"I don't need your pity."

"Wasn't giving you any," he reasoned, folding his

arms as if daring her to argue with him. When she didn't, he went on. "I admire anyone who can take a hit, then pick themselves up and keep on going. You're tougher than you look."

No one had ever spoken to her that way, so directly and with such obvious sincerity. Accustomed to people who fawned or blustered depending on the circumstances, she wasn't sure how to take it. "Thank you?"

"You're welcome. Mind if I ask what happened?"

She winced, but decided that since he seemed determined to work with her, it was easier to get the explanations out of the way sooner rather than later. "In a nutshell, two years ago I was driving back to D.C. and took a shortcut that turned into a patch of ice. Next thing I knew, I woke up strapped into a hospital bed, completely immobilized. They told me I had a fifty-fifty chance of ever walking again."

"Guess you proved them wrong."

"That was the plan."

The response came out more tersely than she'd intended, but Jason didn't seem the least bit fazed. "Good for you."

Flashing her an encouraging smile, he offered his arm, and for some insane reason she took it. The old-fashioned gesture seemed appropriate for him while standing in this old building, dressed like someone who spent his days working hard. Now that she thought about it, he reminded her of the guy on the wrapper of her paper towels.

Only this lumberjack had a real twinkle in his eyes, and he'd managed to get past her usual defenses without any effort at all. That could only mean one thing:

he was trouble. And she'd had enough trouble lately to last her the rest of her life.

Amy Morgan was still the prettiest girl he'd ever seen, Jason thought while he inspected the progress Fred had made on the set pieces. Some were partially assembled, but others lay in a heap backstage with hand-drawn schematics thumbtacked to them. Everything was still in raw form, with no paint or details at all.

It was a big job to complete in only three weeks, and with the holiday shopping season in full swing, it was all hands on deck filling custom orders at the mill in time for Christmas delivery. While he'd much rather be back in Oregon logging, his first obligation was to the family business. It wasn't only Jason and his brother relying on it now. A dozen other people worked there, too, and closing the doors wasn't an option for any of them.

But if he didn't take on Amy's project, who would? Everyone was busy this time of year, and being single, he had more spare hours than most. Each day she spent trying to find a handyman was another day of lost build time. If he didn't step up, when someone finally did it might be too late, and she might have to cancel the show. Some of those kids were probably the same way she'd been, working hard and eager to get their turn in the spotlight. He'd feel awful if they lost out and he could've done something to prevent it.

"I know there's a lot to do," she lamented with a worried look. "Uncle Fred's collision shop just lost a good mechanic to that new chain over in Cambridge, and he's been working extra hours to keep up. He fit this in whenever he could."

"Yeah, it's tough."

She seemed to think he was framing a no, and she stepped forward with desperation clouding her china-doll features. "I can pay you for your time. It wouldn't be much, but you could use it to buy some nice Christmas presents for…whoever."

For some crazy reason, Jason got the feeling she was trying to determine if he was unattached. He couldn't imagine why she cared, but women were funny that way. A guy just asked you straight out if you were seeing someone, while a woman skirted the direct route and snuck in sideways. One of the many reasons he avoided getting tangled up with anyone in particular. He liked his nice, uncomplicated life just the way it was. Drama—especially female drama—he could do without.

Recognizing she was in a tight spot, in the spirit of the season he decided to give her a break and not yank her chain. "My shopping's done, so I don't need the money."

Her dainty mouth fell open in a shocked O. "Are you serious? Everyone needs money."

"I've got a little more than enough." Grinning, he added, "And I don't have a…whoever, so I'm good."

That got her attention, and he watched curiosity flare in those stunning eyes of hers. Crystal-blue, with a lighter burst in the center, they made him think of stars. Wisps of light brown hair had escaped her loose bun, framing her face in a halo of curls. Dressed in pale gray trousers and a white sweater, she brought to mind the angel on top of his parents' Christmas tree.

Dangerous, he cautioned himself. It was okay to admire a woman in a general way, but when he started comparing her to heavenly beings, it was time to take a giant step back and get a grip. Then again, the adorable ballerina she'd once been had stayed in his memory for twenty years. Gazing down at her now, he saw none of the joy on display in the framed photos on the wall. In its place was a lingering sadness that tugged at his heart, making him want to come up with a way to make her smile like that again.

And so, against his better judgment, he held out his hand. "I'm your guy, Amy. I promise not to let you down."

She looked at his hand warily, then said, "The last time a man said that to me, it didn't end so well."

Laced with wry humor, her comment made him laugh. "He was a moron, and if I knew his name, I'd go tell him so."

She studied him for a long moment, then her somber expression lightened just a little. It was such a subtle change, he couldn't help wondering if she'd actually forgotten how to smile. "You know, I believe you. I'm not sure why, but I do."

"About the talking-to or about not letting you down?"

"Both."

Taking his hand, she sealed their deal with a shake that was surprisingly firm for someone so petite. Jason got the distinct impression that something important had just happened to him, but he wasn't exactly sure what it was. One thing was certain: he wouldn't be bored this Christmas.

The thought had just floated through his head when the sound of jingling bells announced another visitor at the front door. When he glanced over, he had to look twice. From where he stood, it looked like a larger-than-life nutcracker in a flashy soldier's uniform was bob-

bing through the large front room on its way toward
the stage. When it got closer, he was relieved to see
that underneath it were very human feet, clad in tie-
dyed sneakers that were a dead giveaway about who'd
come in.

"Hey, you," he greeted Jenna Reed, the town's resi-
dent artist, with a chuckle. "Who's your friend?"

When she set it down, he noticed it was almost as
tall as Amy. "The nutcracker prince, of course. He's
not as big as the signs I made for the sawmill, but he's
got a lot more personality." Turning to Amy, she said,
"I know he's not up to the standards you're used to in
the Big Apple, but what do you think?"

"It's perfect for this show," Amy replied with an approving smile. "And you shouldn't sell yourself short.
This guy is just what I had in mind."

"Awesome." Jenna eyed Jason with curiosity. "No
offense, JB, but I'm used to seeing you out at the mill.
You look a little outta place in here."

"Finishing up Fred's sets."

"I forgot he hurt himself tackling your nephew," she
said to Amy. "How's he doing?"

"Aunt Helen has all she can manage just keeping
him off his feet," Amy explained with a sigh. "The doctor said he needs to take it easy for at least a couple of
weeks. It's only been two days, and he's already driving her crazy."

Jason knew how he'd feel if he was laid up for that
long, and inspiration struck. "Maybe I can knock down
some of the pieces for him to assemble and paint at
home. That'll give him something to do, and your aunt
can keep her sanity."

Amy stared up at him with an expression he couldn't

quite peg, and he worried that he might've overstepped his bounds. Then she gave him a grateful smile, as if he'd come up with the answer to every problem she'd ever faced. Knowing he'd been the one to coax a smile from this troubled woman made him feel like a hero.

"That's brilliant," she said, "but are you sure you want to do that? I mean, you'd be making more work for yourself."

He shrugged. "No big deal. If he's happy, maybe he'll heal up quicker and get back to the garage where he belongs."

"And out of Aunt Helen's hair," she added with a nod. "I like the way you think."

They were still staring at each other when Jenna interrupted with a not-so-subtle cough. When she had their attention, she shook her head. "Are you sure you guys just met?"

"More or less," Jason hedged, figuring Amy wouldn't appreciate him relating their first-meet story from twenty years ago.

"That's funny, 'cause from where I'm standing, you've got that 'known each other awhile' vibe."

"That's crazy," Amy huffed. "Not to mention impossible."

The artist laughed. "I call 'em like I see 'em. Anyway, at least this time you stumbled across one of the good guys."

"I thought they went extinct years ago." There was more than a hint of bitterness in Amy's tone, and he couldn't help wondering what had really happened with her ex. Not that it impacted him in any way, of course. He was just curious.

"Not around here," Jenna corrected her. "I think this is where they all landed."

"I'll have to take your word on that one," Amy retorted as she passed by on her way to somewhere behind the stage that dominated the studio. "I've got your check in the office. I'll be right back."

Once she was out of earshot, Jenna stepped in closer to Jason. "I've gotten to know Amy since she landed here in town this summer, so I'm gonna do you a favor."

Every trace of humor had left her expression, and he returned the somber look. "What kinda favor?"

"Leave the poor girl alone. You're not interested in anything serious, and she's had a really rough time the last couple years. She's not up to any more heartache."

"The accident, you mean."

Jenna's eyes widened in surprise. "She told you?"

When he repeated the gist of his earlier conversation with Amy, Jenna slowly shook her head. "I knew her a month before she told me any of that stuff. How did you get her to open up so fast?"

"It's a knack," he replied with a grin. "People like me."

"Uh-huh. Well, watch yourself, big guy. Amy's been through a lot of twists and turns, and her head's still spinning. The last thing she needs is more trouble."

"Trouble?" he echoed in mock surprise. "From me?"

"Don't get me started," she grumbled, as Amy reappeared at the back of the stage with her check. Jenna took it and without even glancing at it shoved it into the back pocket of her paint-spattered overalls. "Well, kids, it's been fun, but I left my kiln going. The thermostat's busted, so if I don't keep an eye on it, it'll burn my whole studio down. Later."

After the door jingled shut behind her, Amy gave him a knowing feminine look. "She likes you."

"She likes everybody. When you're a freelance artist, it's good for business."

"Are you seriously telling me you're not the least bit interested in her? She's gorgeous and perky, and more fun than any three people I know."

"You're right about all that," he agreed, "which is why Jenna and I are friends. But she treats me like an annoying little brother, and that's fine with me."

"Why? I mean, most guys I know would fall all over themselves to get her attention."

In the cynical comment, he got a glimpse of who Amy had become while she'd been working so hard to establish her career. To his mind, it seemed as if she hadn't enjoyed herself all that much since her early dancing days, at least not on a personal level.

Obviously, she'd spent way too much time with losers who didn't know a remarkable woman when one was standing right in front of them. Sensing an opportunity to distinguish himself from them, he grinned down at her. "Well, I'm not like those guys. Before this show opens, I'm gonna do everything I can to make you believe that."

Her eyes narrowed with suspicion, and she frowned. "You met me an hour ago. Why do you even care?"

"I just do," he replied easily, because he honestly meant it. "But if you need more of a reason, call it Christmas spirit."

With that, he began strolling toward the rear of the stage, stopping when she called out his name. Turning, he said, "Yeah?"

"You're starting now?"

"Molly filled Paul and me up with one of her farmer's breakfasts, so I'm ready to go. Thought I'd start by knocking down some of those bigger pieces that are already put together. Then I'll haul 'em over to Fred's so he can get started painting. Then I'll come back and we can go over whatever plans you've got for getting all this done. Is that okay with you?"

Clearly bewildered by his quick pace, she slowly nodded. "Thank you."

"No problem."

She rewarded him with a timid smile, the kind that could sneak into a man's head and make him forget all kinds of things. Like how he needed to be careful around this woman, because she was fragile and needed time to heal.

The problem was, something about Amy Morgan tugged at the edges of his restless heart in a way no woman ever had. And in spite of his misgivings, he wasn't convinced he should even try to keep her out.

Chapter Two

"She does good work," Amy commented, moving to the side to study the brightly painted nutcracker sign from another angle. "When Jenna and I first got to know each other, I was surprised there was such a talented artist here in Barrett's Mill."

"Must've been nice to find another creative type to hang with out here in the boonies."

He'd nailed her feelings so exactly, she gaped at him in amazement. With his rugged appearance and carefree attitude, she'd never have guessed he'd be so perceptive. It made her wonder what other qualities might be hiding behind that wide-open grin.

Pushing those very personal observations from her mind, she dragged herself back to the task at hand. "I have to start advertising the show right away, so I'd like to get this guy set up out front. Would you mind helping with that?"

"'Course not." Picking up the sign, he tucked it under his arm and motioned her past. "After you."

The rough-and-tumble streets of Washington and New York had left her accustomed to fending for herself. Men didn't typically defer to her this way, and she found his gentlemanly gesture charming. *Southern boys,* she mused as she walked through the studio. She could get used to this.

Out front, she stopped to the left of the door. "I thought he'd look best here, next to the window. What do you think?"

That got her a bright, male laugh, the kind that sounded as if it got plenty of use. "I'm about as far from a decorator as you can get. Lumber, saws, hammers, that's me. You're better off following your own gut on this one."

His innocent comment landed on her bruised heart like a fist, reminding her of the last time she'd followed her gut—and the unmitigated disaster it had led her into. If only she'd kept to her original course instead of taking that shortcut, she'd still be on her way to becoming principal ballerina for an international company. Never again would she deviate from the plan, she promised herself for the hundredth time. Improvising had cost her everything.

Swallowing her exaggerated reaction to his advice, she focused on identifying the perfect location for her sign. Jason set it in place, and she considered it for a moment, then shook her head. "Jenna made him double-sided on purpose, and I want to make sure people get a good view of him from the sidewalk and the street. The idea is to draw them in so they'll look at the other decorations and the playbill in the window. Try angling him this way."

Demonstrating with her hands, she waited and then reassessed. "Now he's too much toward the studio."

After several more attempts, Jason plunked the sign

on the paved walkway and rested an arm on top of his Cossack's helmet. "You're kidding, right? We've tipped this thing every way but upside down. You're seriously telling me we haven't hit the right spot yet?"

"There's no point in doing something imperfectly," she shot back in self-defense.

He gazed at her thoughtfully, and she got the eerie feeling he could see things she'd rather keep to herself. "That doesn't sound like something someone our age would say. Who taught you that?"

"My mother. And she's right, by the way. Perfection is the only goal for a balleri—ballet teachers."

In a heartbeat, his confused expression shifted to one of sympathy, and he frowned. "You were gonna say *ballerina,* weren't you?"

"I misspoke. Now, are you going to help me finish this, or should I do it myself?"

He opened his mouth, then closed it and shook his head. "You don't want folks feeling sorry for you, I get that. Your life's taken a nasty turn, and I respect what you're doing to get it back together." Moving a step closer, he added, "But you're here now, and you don't have to do everything on your own anymore. Folks in Barrett's Mill are real fond of your aunt and uncle, and they're gonna want to help you, whether you like it or not."

"Including you?"

Warmth spread through his features, burnishing the gold in his eyes to a color she'd never seen before. When he finally smiled, for the first time in her life, she actually felt her knees begin quivering. If he took it into his head to kiss her, she was fairly certain she wouldn't have the strength—or the will—to stop him.

"Including me," he said so quietly, she almost didn't hear him.

Struggling to keep her head clear, she pulled her dignity around her like a shield. "That's really not necessary. I'm very capable of taking care of myself, and I didn't get where I am by letting people poke their noses into my life and tell me what to do."

Mischief glinted in his eyes, and he chuckled. "Me, neither."

Because of her size, Amy was accustomed to being misjudged, underestimated and generally dismissed by others. Sometimes it actually worked to her advantage, lulling people into a harmless perception of her that masked her relentless determination until she was ready to bring it out into the open. By then, it was too late for whoever had dared to step in between her and whatever she wanted.

But Jason Barrett, with his country-boy looks and disarming personality, didn't seem inclined to follow along. Instead, he'd taken stock of her and had apparently come to the conclusion that she didn't scare him in the least. She'd given it her best shot, and it had sailed wide. So far wide, in fact, that the only sensible thing left to do was admit defeat.

"Okay, you win. This time," she added, pointing a stern finger at him in warning. "But Arabesque is my business, and things around here will be run my way. Got it?"

"Yes, ma'am." Tacking on yet another maddening grin, he went on. "But I've got an idea about how to balance this entrance display. If you're done scolding me, would you like to hear it?"

The concept of someone her size hassling the brawny

carpenter was absurd, and she got the distinct impression he was trying to get her to lighten up. Since he was bending over backward to be entertaining, she decided the least she could do was smile. "Sure. Go ahead."

Propping the nutcracker in place against a shrub, he moved to the other side of the walkway that led to the studio's glass front door. Holding out his arms, he said, "Imagine a nicely decorated Christmas tree over here. Then you could do narrow pillars with an arch over the top strung with lights and a sign telling people when the show is."

"I don't think Jenna has time to do another sign for me."

"It's just lettering," he pointed out. "I'll get some stencils and knock it out in no time."

Squinting, she envisioned what he'd described. Since the sun went down so much earlier this time of year, people running errands on Main Street after work would be drawn to Arabesque, just the way she was hoping. They'd come over to check out the cheery display window and get a look inside the freshly redecorated studio. Not only would it boost attendance for *The Nutcracker,* it might gain her some new students. Profits were the name of the new game she was playing, and anything that had the potential to bring in customers was worth a try.

"I like it," she announced. "When do you think you can have it done?"

"How's Monday afternoon sound?"

She had no idea how much work was involved in what he'd described, but he sounded so confident, she didn't even consider questioning the quick turnaround. "Perfect. Thank you."

Plunging his hands into the front pockets of his well-worn jeans, he said, "I oughta warn you, it probably won't be perfect. But I can promise you it'll be good enough to do the job."

"Like you?"

"And you." Slinging the wooden soldier over his shoulder, he gazed down at her. "For most of us, that's enough."

"Not for me," she assured him. "I don't stop until whatever I'm doing can't possibly be any better."

"We've all got flaws, y'know. It's what we accomplish in spite of 'em that makes us who we are."

The last thing she'd have expected this morning was to find herself in a philosophical debate with a guy carrying a life-size nutcracker. "That's a nice thought, but some of us are more imperfect than others. It keeps us from being our best."

"Maybe that's 'cause you're meant to be something else."

Clearly, he meant for his calm, rational explanation to make her feel better about her lingering injuries. He didn't mention God by name, but the silver cross on the chain around his neck filled in the blanks nicely for her. While she respected his right to hold that faith, his comment sparked a flame of resentment she fought to control. "Maybe I wanted the chance to choose for myself."

All her life, she'd done everything her Sunday-school teacher had taught her to do. She went to church, said all the prayers, sang all the hymns. She'd worked relentlessly to polish the talent God gave her until it shone as brightly as any stage lights in the world.

And then He took it all away.

Lying in that lonely hospital bed, she begged Him

to help her, to make everything the way it was before. And what happened? Nothing.

She didn't trust herself to speak calmly right now, but from the sympathy in Jason's eyes, she might as well have told him her whole tragic story.

"We don't always get what we ask for, Amy."

"Tell me about it."

More worked up than she'd been in a long, long time, she marched away from him and yanked open the door to escape into the only part of her world she still understood.

The rest of his day at Arabesque passed by in silence. Except when he was hammering or drilling, anyway. Other than that, Amy avoided him with a deftness that impressed and saddened him all at the same time. He'd been around enough wounded people in his life to recognize the regret that trailed after her, darkening her eyes with the kind of unrelenting sorrow he could only begin to imagine.

He'd just met her, but he instinctively wanted to do whatever he could to pound down the road ahead of her to make it easier for her to walk. The women who usually appealed to him were engaging, uncomplicated types who didn't eat much and laughed easily. Something told him Amy Morgan was complicated by nature, which should've been an enormous red flag for him.

Unfortunately, it only made him wonder what it would take to make her laugh. Then again, he thought as he packed Fred's tools into their cases, maybe he was getting ahead of himself. After all, he'd barely been able to tease a smile out of her, and they'd been together most of the day.

Stopping by her office, he knocked on the frame of the open door. "Everything's put away, so I'm gonna get outta here before your students show up. I'll be back Monday with those extra pieces we talked about."

"Thank you."

"No problem. Have a good rehearsal."

Since he was out of things to say, he waved and began backing away. When she called out his name, he paused in the hallway. "Yeah?"

"Things were so hectic today, we never settled on your hourly rate."

"I thought we agreed on zero."

Narrowing her eyes, she tilted her head in a skeptical pose he suspected was fairly common for her. "I assumed you were joking about that."

"Nope. I'm sure Fred wasn't charging you, so since I'm filling in for him, it wouldn't be right for me to do it."

"Where I'm from, strangers don't do things for nothing."

"Huh," he said with his brightest grin. "And here I thought we were friends."

While he watched, the brittle cynicism fell away, and the corner of her mouth lifted in a wry grin. "I should warn you, I'm not the easiest person to be friends with."

"That's cool. I like a challenge."

Before she could warp their light exchange into something heavier, he turned and headed for the front door, whistling "Jingle Bell Rock" as he went. When the orchestral holiday medley coming over the studio speakers increased in volume, he knew she'd heard him and was registering her disapproving opinion of his taste in Christmas music. Didn't matter a bit to him, he thought as he stepped from the studio. So they didn't enjoy the same kind of tunes. It wasn't as if he was going to marry her or anything.

Outside, he paused to take in the view of his hometown at the holidays. While he'd been gone, he'd seen plenty of towns, big, small and everything in between. He recalled most of their names, but none had ever measured up to Barrett's Mill for him. At first glance, this Main Street resembled so many others, lined with buildings constructed in a time when skilled craftsmen took great pride in building things that would last forever.

The structures had a solid look to them, which gave the village a quaint, old-fashioned appeal for residents and visitors alike. Especially this time of year, when each business went all out to win the Chamber of Commerce award for best commercial decorations. The jewelry store's front window was dominated by a glacial scene that had sparkling rings and earrings pinned into the fake waterfall. Next to it, a shop that sold office supplies had set up a huge pile of brightly wrapped gifts, with a few open at the front to display the latest gadgets you could find inside. Every window was rimmed in lights, and on a cloudy day like today they gave off a cheerful glow that looked like something straight out of a holiday movie.

Across the width of the street, volunteers had strung the lighted garlands and wreaths the same way they'd done for generations. For as long as Jason could remember, when those festive greens went up, he knew Christmas was right around the corner. Even when he'd lived out West, he'd come back home every year, even if it was only for a few days. As he got older, reconnecting with those lifelong memories comforted him, no matter what might have gone wrong for him elsewhere.

He recognized a few of the people out window-shopping and lifted a hand in greeting before climbing into his truck. Actually, it was one of the mill trucks, older than dirt and held together by rust and a lot of prayers. Paul had gotten it running over the summer and offered it to Jason when he finally broke down and bought a pickup manufactured in this century. To start it, Jason usually needed a screwdriver and a boatload of patience. Since it hadn't been idle all that long, he took his chances and turned the key. Nothing happened at first, but when he gave it another shot, the engine whined a bit and caught. Pumping the gas pedal, he let the motor settle into the throaty rumble that told him it would keep running long enough for him to get where he was going. Usually.

As he made his way toward the edge of town, the pavement gave way to gravel, and he turned in by the sign Jenna had made to mark the very first business in town: Barrett's Sawmill, Est. 1866. He felt a quick jolt of pride, recalling how his older brother, Paul, had left his wandering ways behind and come back to re-open the bankrupt family business. Now a humming custom-furniture manufacturer, they made things by hand the old-fashioned way, in a mill powered by its original waterwheel.

It was a far cry from the lumber camps Jason had been working at the past couple of years. About half as exciting, he mused as he parked next to Chelsea's silver convertible, but way safer. Before he'd even closed the driver's door, baying echoed from behind the mill house, and a huge red bloodhound raced out to meet him.

"Hey there, Boyd." He laughed as the dog leaped up to give him the canine version of a high five. "What's shakin'?"

The dog barked in reply, letting him go and racing around him in circles all the way up to the front porch. Inside, Jason paused outside the office's half door and waved in at his newest sister-in-law. "Hey, Chelsea. How're the numbers looking this week?"

Beaming, she gave him an enthusiastic thumbs-up. "I love Christmas shoppers. They need things fast, and they're willing to pay extra for quick delivery."

Jason groaned, only half joking. "Sounds like we're gonna get real busy."

"I wouldn't take up any new hobbies," Paul advised from the open sliding door that led into the rear of the mill. Wiping grease from his hands on a rag, he went on. "This is supposed to be your last Saturday off till the end of the year. What're you doing here?"

"Making a Christmas tree."

Chelsea laughed. "Doesn't God already take care of that?"

While Jason explained what he was up to, he kept things vague to avoid creating the wrong impression about his situation with Amy. Despite his best efforts, though, Paul's expression grew increasingly suspicious.

"Uh-huh." Dragging it out longer than usual, he folded his arms in disapproval. "Now, how 'bout the truth?"

"That *is* the truth," Jason insisted, as much for himself as his nosy brother. "The lady wants a tree and a nice arch overtop, so I'm making them for her. And for the kids. They're working hard on their show, and they deserve a big audience. I figured it's a nice, Christmassy thing to do."

"It's very nice." With her kitten, Daisy, cradled in her arms, Chelsea came out to back him up. Sending a stern look at her husband, she smiled at Jason. "I'm sure she really appreciates your help."

"Don't encourage him," Paul cautioned her. "He's got a weakness for pretty faces and sad stories."

"I do not," Jason protested. Paul raised an eyebrow at him, and he decided it was pointless to argue. "Okay, you're right, but this time's different."

"How?"

He didn't want to lie, but it wasn't his place to air her personal history, so he hedged, "Amy was advertising for a carpenter to replace Fred, and the job's easy enough. Everyone else in the family does work for the church or charities this time of year, and I've been looking for a way to pitch in somewhere."

"You've been doing that ever since you moved in with Gram and Granddad." Paul rested a hand on his shoulder with a proud smile. "His cancer's getting worse every day, and she needs your help after Mom goes home for the night. We're all grateful to you for stepping up like that."

The praise settled well, and Jason smiled back. "That's why this project is so great. Working at Amy's, I'll be five minutes away if they need me. The show's the week before Christmas, so my part'll be over soon enough."

"You realize you're doing an awful lot of work for a woman you met—" Pausing, he chuckled. "When did you meet her, anyway?"

"This morning, after you and I had breakfast at the

Whistlestop. She was decorating out front of the dance place, and since she's new in town, I went over to say hi." When Paul leveled one of those big-brother looks at him, Jason let out a frustrated growl. "You're acting like I proposed or something."

"Well…"

"That was a long time ago," Jason reminded him, poking him in the chest for emphasis. "I learned my lesson with her, and I've got no plans for making that mistake again anytime soon."

"I have to ask," Chelsea interrupted. "Who on earth are you talking about?"

"Rachel McCarron," Jason replied with a wry grin. "It didn't work out."

"That little minx took off with your best friend and your truck," Paul reminded him, as if he'd lost his memory or something. "Oh, and the ring. Nice girl."

"Whatever."

Paul opened his mouth, then closed it almost immediately. Jason didn't understand why until he noticed the chilly stare Paul was getting from his wife. It reminded him of Amy's disapproving looks, and he smothered a grin. He'd never had the opportunity to compare one woman with another this way. If he could somehow figure out what was going on in their heads, it might actually be entertaining.

"Fine." With a look that was half smile and half grimace, Paul stepped back to let Jason into the working area of the mill. "Whattaya need?"

Chapter Three

Monday morning crept by at a pace that would have embarrassed the slowest turtle on earth. Banished to her office at the rear of the studio by her carpenter, Amy chafed impatiently and tried not to check the old schoolhouse clock on the wall every two seconds.

She was dying to see what he'd come up with for the entryway. Before she went completely bonkers, she decided it was better to distract herself until he was finished. She could use the free time to inventory her costume collection, assessing what Aunt Helen had on hand so she could determine what they needed to buy for the cast.

Because the studio had been built on her aunt's stellar reputation as a dance instructor, Amy had insisted Aunt Helen remain a silent partner in the business. So every decision was a "they" situation, which was new for someone who'd spent most of her life focused on her own career. It was one of many changes Amy had encountered since coming back to Barrett's Mill after so many years away.

Like Jason Barrett.

The man couldn't be any more different from her ex, and she couldn't help but compare the two. A dancer himself, Devon hadn't been able to cope with the somber prospect of being shackled to a wife who was so limited physically. He bolted shortly after her grim final diagnosis, taking his great-grandmother's engagement ring with him.

Since then, the men who'd crossed her path had been either medical professionals or old friends who viewed her as more of a younger sister than a romantic interest. Heartbroken by Devon's betrayal, her new hands-off status with the male species actually suited her just fine. She had no intention of letting another one close enough to hurt her by taking off just when she needed him most.

Not that Jason fell into that category, she reminded herself as she eased out of her chair. In a few short days, he'd proven himself not only respectful but dependable, two qualities she valued in anyone. On her way into the storeroom, she made several attempts to classify him based on other guys she'd known, but came up empty. Then she heard his teasing voice in her mind.

And here I thought we were friends.

Smiling to herself, she decided he was indeed her friend, one she might enjoy getting to know better. After all, she mused as she began pairing up satin slippers, you never knew when a big, strong carpenter might come in handy.

From the doorway, she heard a low whistle and turned to find him staring into the oversize closet. "It looks like a cotton-candy machine blew up in here."

The comment was so spot-on, she couldn't help

laughing. "I guess it does. That's what happens when you cast too many sugar-plum fairies."

"How many extra do you have?"

Glancing up, she quickly did the math. "Ten, I think."

"Why didn't you just make them something else? Save yourself a little netting?"

"Because all the girls wanted to be Clara or a sugar-plum fairy. For this production, no one's en pointe, and only Heidi Peterson could manage the basics for Clara. That means I need lots of these," she added, fluffing the layers of pink tulle hanging on the rack.

Something in his expression shifted, and he took a step inside the cramped room. "You mean, you adjusted the traditional cast so they could play the roles they wanted?"

"Of course. They're kids, and it's Christmas." Baffled by his reaction to her scaled-down production, she frowned. "Why?"

"Because that's the last thing I'd expect from a perfectionist like you."

The gold in his eyes glittered with an emotion she couldn't begin to define, and she found herself caught up in the hypnotic warmth of his gaze. He didn't move toward her, but his imposing presence filled the room with something that was more than physical. In a jolt of understanding, she recognized that it came from a heart so generous, he'd volunteered his time and talents to a stranger simply because she needed his help. Instinctively, she knew he was someone who treated people well as a matter of principle, not as a means to an end.

The kind of man who'd treasure the woman fortunate enough to be the one he loved.

That realization struck her with a certainty so powerful, it actually knocked her back a step. Trying to regain her perspective, she dragged her eyes away and made a show of hunting for the slipper that matched the one still clutched in her hand. "Did you need something?"

"Your stamp of approval." Cocking his arm, he offered it to her with a bright grin. "Wanna come see?"

She did, very much, but she was hesitant to take his arm. Since she couldn't come up with a way to refuse it politely, she fell back on logic. "That's sweet, but we can't fit through that door side by side."

"Got me there. Ladies first, then."

The way he kept referring to her as a lady made Amy want to giggle, and she firmly tamped down the impulse. He was obviously trying to charm her, but it would work only if she let it. She'd handled many situations like this in the past, and she was well aware that keeping him at a safe distance was the best approach.

But it wasn't half as much fun as going along, she admitted with a muted sigh. Being sensible could be such a killjoy. Before they turned the corner to enter the front section of the studio, he abruptly stopped walking.

"Is something wrong?" she asked, standing on tiptoe to look past him. Big as he was, she couldn't see a thing, and she started to worry. "It all fell down, didn't it?"

"That's insulting," he informed her with a good-natured chuckle, "but since you don't know me very well, I'll let you get by with it. Close your eyes."

"Why?"

"So you'll be surprised."

He said that as if it should have been obvious to her, and she felt a twinge of regret for not sharing his enthusiasm for what he'd built. She was the one who'd asked him to do it, and she knew she should be more excited. Sadly, since her dream of dancing had ended up wrapped around a light pole outside D.C., it was all she could do to keep trudging forward.

"I'm not very fond of surprises," she said as evenly as she could manage. "I much prefer it when things go according to plan."

Most of the people she knew would bristle at that or chide her for being a control freak. But not this guy. Instead, he gave her an encouraging smile. "My sister-in-law, Chelsea, used to be like that before Paul showed her how much fun she was missing."

"I don't see what that has to do with me."

"Just that folks can change, is all. Now, close your eyes."

She couldn't understand why it meant so much to him, but he'd put in a lot of work and hadn't charged her a dime. The least she could do was humor him. "Okay, they're closed."

Unfortunately, that threw off her equilibrium, and she felt as if she was going to fall. The sensation was alarming, and she clutched his arm more tightly to maintain her balance. It reminded her of the torturous first steps after the surgery that had shored up her spine but ended her career, and she felt a cold sweat breaking out on her face.

"You're all right, Amy," Jason murmured in a gentle drawl near her ear. "I've got you."

Sure enough, he was bracing her with one strong arm, and she was stunned to find it wasn't scary at all. Not trusting herself to speak without a whimper, she nodded and let him lead her through the studio and out the front door.

Crisp, cool air greeted her, and she fought off a shiver

that had nothing to do with the weather. That was the scent she'd noticed on Jason the first day they met, fresh and outdoorsy. Something told her that from now on whenever she was caught outside on a winter day, she'd think of him.

Deliberately pulling her mind back to practical things, she asked, "Can I look now?"

"Go ahead."

She opened her eyes, then blinked in total disbelief. He'd mentioned something about adding a tree and an archway, but this was way beyond anything she could have imagined even on her best day.

The simple arch she'd envisioned had become a full-fledged arbor, twined with greenery and twinkling white lights. The tree wasn't made of wood, but was a seven-foot-tall artificial spruce with more lights and a multipointed crystal star on top. Gifts wrapped in gold and silver paper were clustered around the base, and one box looked as if it had spilled open to show off a collection of wooden soldiers like the ones that would march onstage in a few short weeks.

On the left side was her nutcracker. Sort of. The static sign Jenna had made now swung from hooks that allowed it to move in the breeze. The new arrangement made him look as if he was dancing. Awestruck by the combined effect of all those Christmassy elements, she was convinced a professional designer couldn't have devised a better representation of the popular holiday ballet.

Apparently, there was more to the towering lumberjack than axes and hammers. Who would have guessed that? Astounded by the results, she stared up at Jason in disbelief. "You did this?"

"Yup." Folding his arms, he cocked his head with an eager expression. "You like it?"

"Are you kidding? I love it!" Forgetting her vow to remain detached, she laughed and gave him a quick hug. "It must've taken you forever. How did you manage to get so much done over the weekend?"

"The tree I made didn't turn out so well. Then I remembered your aunt used to put one up. I found it out back in your storage shed."

"You mean, the one that's locked and I can't find the key to?"

"That's the one."

"How did you get it open?" As soon as she finished her question, she had to laugh. "Let me guess. Sledgehammer?"

"Bolt cutters, and I replaced the lock with a new one. The keys are in your office." Glancing around, he leaned in and murmured, "I made the arbor for my gram's garden. I'm gonna need that back before Christmas."

Impressed beyond words, she went up to examine it more closely. Flowers and vines were carved into every piece of wood, curling up to meet in the middle of the arch in a heart with a script *B* in the center. "Jason, this is absolutely beautiful. You're incredibly talented."

He gave her an aw-shucks grin that made him look like an overgrown little boy. "I'm sure you're used to fancier stuff, so it's nice of you to say that. The power box is down here." He pointed to an open-back square of wood. "The cord runs to your outside receptacle by the front door, and I marked the switch in the lobby that controls it. That way, you can turn everything on and off from inside."

She was amazed that he'd thought to set it up so she

wouldn't have to go out in the cold to shut things down. They barely knew each other, and already he'd come up with a way to make her life easier—and warmer. After fending for herself for so long, she liked knowing he was looking out for her.

Despite her usual reserve, she could no longer deny she was warming up to this irresistible man. "Jason, I don't know what to say. This is way beyond what I was expecting. How can I ever repay you?"

"Another one of those hugs would be cool."

Laughing because she couldn't help herself, she obliged him, adding a peck on his cold cheek for good measure. Pulling away, she frowned. "You must be freezing, after working out here so long. Would you like some coffee or something to warm you up?"

"That'd be great, thanks."

"I don't have any made in the office right now, but there's some out back. Come on."

Again, he motioned for her to go in ahead of him. For years, she'd been living in big, bustling cities where everyone rushed past her as if she didn't exist. It might be old-fashioned of her, but she had to admit she liked Jason's way better.

Amy's apartment was...not what he'd expected.

Raised by his parents to be respectful above all else, Jason stood awkwardly in the middle of the narrow doorway, trying to come up with something nice to say. Built onto the rear of the studio, it was a single room with a tiny kitchenette and a small bathroom. The walls were raw drywall, and several buckets scattered around the floor alerted him there were leaks in the roof. Unfortunately, that wasn't the worst part. "There's something wrong with the furnace back here. I've been in freezers warmer than this."

"You have not," she scoffed.

"I worked for a butcher in Utah for six months, and trust me, his cooler temp wasn't far off this place. How do I get to your utilities?" She blinked up at him, then began casting around as if she had no clue. It shouldn't have been funny, but he couldn't help laughing. "There must be a way to get into the crawl space under the addition. Do you know where it is?"

"I'm sure Uncle Fred does."

Jason hated to bother the man for something that simple, and he shrugged. "No problem. I'll find it."

"That's not necessary. I'm hardly ever in here, so it doesn't bother me."

"Must get cold at night, though."

After a couple of moments, she relented with a sigh. "Okay, you got me. I sleep on the couch in the office."

"That can't be good for your back," he chided her as gently as he could. With an injury like hers, she should have the most supportive mattress she could get, not some lumpy old sofa. "You keep doing that, pretty soon you won't be able to get up in the morning."

"It's fine," she said curtly.

"It's not fine, and before I go, I'll make sure you've got heat. While we're at it, have you got any idea where your roof's leaking from?"

"Umm…above?"

A smart aleck, he groaned silently. Just what he needed. Then again, he'd had more fun with her than any other woman he'd met recently. He wasn't entirely sure what that meant, and fortunately, he didn't have time to ponder it now. "I'll climb up there, too, and find out what's going on. My hunch is you lost a few shingles in that bad storm we had last week, and now the water's getting in. There's some extra roofing stuff in the shed, so I'll do a patch that'll keep things dry in here."

Gratitude flooded her eyes, and she gave him a sweet but cautious smile. "Thank you."

Something in the way she said it got to him, and it took him a minute to figure out why. When he landed on an explanation, he couldn't keep back a grin. Troubled but unwilling to ask for help, her fierce sense of pride reminded him of himself. "I'm confused. Why're you living like this when your aunt and uncle are right here in town?"

"I prefer having my own place, even if it's not ideal."

Her suddenly cool tone warned him not to push, and he decided it would be wise to let her have this one. It was none of his business anyway, so he focused on something less personal. "So, we've got the furnace and the roof. What else is wrong?"

"I hate to impose on you," she hedged, handing him a bright red cup with a handle molded to resemble a candy cane. "You're already doing so much for me."

He didn't think this serious and very independent woman would respond well to a damsel-in-distress joke, so he sipped his coffee and saluted her with the festive mug. "'Tis the season and all."

Another hesitation, then she finally gave in and rattled off a list of problems, from leaky plumbing to some kind of vague fluttery sound above the drop ceiling.

"I'd imagine there's a bird stuck in there," he commented. "Or a bat."

Every bit of color drained from her face, and he reached out to steady her in case she fainted on him.

After a few moments, she seemed to collect herself and pulled back. "Bats?"

"Kidding." Sort of. But her reaction had been real enough, and he made a mental note that the pretty ballerina wasn't a big fan of the local wildlife.

"I do not want anything flying or crawling or scurrying around where I live," she announced very clearly.

"Don't worry. If I can't get rid of 'em myself, I'll call an exterminator."

"But don't hurt them," she amended, her soft heart reflected in those stunning blue eyes. "Just take them out to the country where they belong."

"Will do." While they chatted, he'd been eyeballing the old floorboards, searching for some kind of opening. When he located it in the kitchen, he popped the edge with the heel of his boot and set it aside. "Got a flashlight?"

That she had, and after she gave it to him, he swung it around in the darkness. The opening was a pretty tight fit for a guy his size, but he decided to give it a shot. Worst case, he'd get stuck and Paul would come rescue him. And never let him hear the end of it.

Thinking again, he handed his phone over to Amy. "There's gonna be some banging and grumbling down there, so don't worry. If I'm not back in ten minutes, call my dad and tell him to bring a reciprocating saw. His name is Tom, and he's speed-dial number 2."

"Reciprocating saw," she repeated with an efficient nod. "Got it."

"I don't suppose you've got a pair of pliers or a wrench or anything?"

To his amazement, she went to an upper cupboard and brought out a small toolbox. "Uncle Fred left me this in case I needed something. Will anything in there help you?"

"Maybe." Jason took what he thought would be most helpful and tucked the tools into the back pockets of his jeans. Then he sat on the edge of the opening and gave her a mock salute. "Here goes nothin'."

He wedged himself into the cramped space and pulled himself along on his back, hand over hand from one floor joist to the next. When light suddenly flooded the darkness, he yelped in surprise. "Whoa! What'd you do?"

"I wheeled in a portable spotlight from the studio," she replied in a voice muffled by the floor. "Is it helping at all, or should I change the angle?"

"It's awesome," he approved heartily. "Thanks."

"You're welcome."

Even from a distance, she sounded pretty proud of herself, and he chuckled. To his relief, the furnace malfunction was nothing more than an air duct that had wiggled loose and was dangling free. He nearly shouted out the problem, then thought better of it. From several comments she'd made, he gathered Amy was concerned about money. She probably wouldn't be thrilled to discover she'd been paying to heat the crawl space under her apartment.

Reaching into his pocket, he fished out a screwdriver and tightened the screws on the collar that fastened the duct in place.

One extra turn for good measure, Jason. He heard Granddad's voice in his memory. That kind of thing happened more often lately, as Will Barrett's time on earth gradually ticked away. Swallowing the lump that had suddenly formed in his throat, Jason grimaced even as he followed his grandfather's advice.

When he was finished, he carefully shimmied back out the way he'd come in, settling on Amy's kitchen floor in a cloud of dust. "Sorry about that."

"Don't be silly," she scolded with a delighted expression. "Do you feel that? It's warm air!"

Grabbing his hand, she held it over a nearby register to prove it. When their eyes met, she seemed to realize what she'd done and abruptly let go. Feeling slightly awkward, he did his best not to read anything into the odd exchange. She'd been freezing, and he was the one who fixed her furnace. No biggie.

But another part of him saw things differently. Until now, she'd been polite but reserved with him, making him believe it would take a long time—and a truckload of patience—to gain her trust. That quick but impulsive gesture told him he was making progress, and she was beginning to warm up to him.

He didn't know what the lady had in mind, but he was looking forward to finding out.

Chapter Four

Rehearsals with her little troupe of dancers were always interesting.

Having been involved with professional dance companies for most of her life, Amy had to frequently remind herself these were kids in a small town whose first exposure to ballet was coming through her. Her purpose in starting with *The Nutcracker* was twofold: it had a nice story and it had an unlimited number of roles available. When they were finished, she hoped her students loved it as much as she did.

But for now, she'd give anything to get Brad Knowlton to pay attention long enough to absorb the set blocking she'd just explained for the umpteenth time. "This is your mark," she repeated as patiently as she could. "We taped it here last week, remember?"

His eight-year-old face wrinkled into a frown, and if he'd been a grown-up, she would've assumed he really was trying to cooperate, but his mind was elsewhere. Since this was her first formal experience with teaching, she wasn't sure what the problem was. So she took a stab at identifying whatever was troubling her

nutcracker prince. Clapping her hands to get their attention, she announced, "Let's take a break, everyone.
Get a snack, use the bathroom and meet me back onstage in ten minutes."

That was one trick she'd learned the first day with
her raucous crew. They loved being on the big stage,
with its many spotlights overhead, and its triple rows
of elegant velvet draperies that could be opened and
closed as needed. Giggling and chatting excitedly, they
went off in a more or less orderly line to get cookies
and juice from the small fridge she always kept stocked
with treats. Teaching dance to kids under the age of
twelve was kind of like being a lion tamer, she mused
with a smile. It never hurt to keep some of their favorite foods close by.

She let them all go ahead of her, then helped herself to a bottle of water. The cookies looked yummy,
but her lingering injuries limited her physical activity,
and she had to keep an eagle eye on her weight. Slight
as she was, if she gained too many pounds, her recon-
structed back and spine would pay the price, and she'd
be in major trouble. As with most things, she'd learned
that the hard way.

Averting her eyes from the temptation, she took a
seat next to Brad, who'd crammed a chocolate-chip
cookie into his mouth and stacked three more on his
napkin in the shape of a pyramid. While he chewed, she
casually asked, "Having a good time tonight?"

Still munching, he swallowed and then nodded. His
brown eyes looked unsure, though, and she edged a
little closer. "You're not really, are you?"

After hesitating for a moment, he shook his head and
sipped some juice. Since he didn't seem eager to con-

fide in her, Amy debated whether to let it go. She hated it when people forced her to talk, but with the days to opening night ticking down like an Advent calendar, she didn't have much choice. If Brad didn't want to play the lead, she had to find another boy who did ASAP.

She tried to put herself in his place but discovered even her vivid imagination wasn't that good. She'd never been a young boy, after all. What did she know about how their brains worked?

Hoping she wouldn't come across to him as a disapproving adult, she began her inquisition. "You seemed to be having fun with this the last time we rehearsed. Did something happen between then and now to make you change your mind?"

While he considered her question, she fought the urge to step in and help him make the right choice. Patience wasn't exactly her strong point, but she tamped down her anxiety and summoned an understanding smile. She didn't want to lose him, but she only wanted him to remain in the cast if he was enjoying himself. This was supposed to be fun, and she didn't want any of the kids to feel pressured.

Finally, he said, "My mom took me to see *The Nutcracker* this weekend."

"What a great idea! How did you like it?"

"It was awesome," he replied, eyes wide with enthusiasm. "The soldiers and battle stuff were really cool. They shot off a cannon, and the prince got to kill the mouse king with his sword. How come we're not doing that?"

Boys and their toys, she thought, muting a grin that would only insult him. His mother probably wanted to expose him to some culture, and his takeaway was the battle scene. "First of all, I don't own a cannon, so that was out. Secondly, I wanted to keep our show short enough for little kids in the audience to enjoy. You have a two-year-old sister. How long can she sit still?"

"Not very long," he admitted. "But having a sword would be cool."

She could envision it now: the nutcracker prince chasing flowers and sugar-plum fairies all over her studio, waving a blade over his head like some marauding pirate captain. In an attempt to avoid being the bad guy on this issue, she asked, "How do you think your mother would like that?"

His hopeful expression deflated, and he stared down at the table with a sigh. "She'd hate it. She'd say I could poke someone's eye out or something stupid like that."

"I'm sure you wouldn't hurt anyone on purpose, but accidents can happen when there are so many people onstage together. Someone could stumble and poke themselves, and then we'd be in trouble."

"I guess."

He was one of a handful of boys she taught, and by far the most talented. With a wiry, athletic build, he seemed to genuinely enjoy learning the routines, and he had a natural stage presence rare in someone his age. Because of that, she hated seeing him so disheartened and searched for a way to ease his disappointment.

Inspiration struck, and she suggested, "Why don't we both think about it and come up with something else cool for your character to have? Maybe we could add something to your costume that would make you stand out more from the other soldiers, or give you a solo dance in the spotlight without Clara."

She could almost hear the very proper Russian choreographer she'd last worked with shrieking in horror, but Amy put aside her artistic sensibilities and focused on Brad. If adding a quick progression for him would make him happy, she'd gladly do it. The success of Arabesque hinged on keeping her students—and their parents—coming back for more lessons and recitals. While this wasn't the performing career she'd dreamed of, at least by teaching she was still involved in dancing.

She didn't know how to do anything else, so if the studio failed she'd have no other options. When she let herself think about it, she got so nervous she could hardly breathe. So for now, she blocked out the scary possibilities and waited for Brad's answer.

After what felt like forever, he met her eyes and gave her a little grin. "Can I jump like the prince I saw this weekend? It was like he was flying."

This boy was far from a full grand jeté, but she didn't bother pointing that out. Instead, she nodded. "It'll take some extra work, but I think you can do it. What do you say?"

"Sure. Thanks, Miss Morgan."

She was so relieved, she almost hugged him, then thought better of it. She'd learned that boys were funny about that kind of thing, and she didn't want to destroy the rapport she was building with him by overstepping her boundaries. Instead, she held up her fist for a bump like she'd seen him do with his buddies. "You're welcome. We're due back in a couple of minutes, so finish up."

"Yes, ma'am."

He chugged the rest of his drink, then bolted for the bathroom. Glancing around at the rest of her class, she noticed how cheerful they seemed to be. Here, with their friends, surrounded by the Christmas setting she'd painstakingly designed to invoke the spirit of the ballet they were learning. It was almost time to get back to work, so she picked up her water and slowly moved toward the stage. On her way, she passed the photo Jason had pointed out during his first visit, and while she normally ignored those old pictures, this time she felt compelled to stop and look.

And remember.

For most of her life, she'd spent the holidays onstage, in the background as part of the supporting cast and later as Clara, twirling with her nutcracker and later meeting up with her prince. During the curtain call, she'd look out to find her mother in the audience, proudly leading the standing ovations, a huge bouquet of pink roses and baby's breath in her arms. From her first production to her last, Mom had always been there, dancing every step with her, tears of joy shining in her eyes.

What would she think of this one? Amy wondered. With her daughter in the wings, adjusting costumes and fetching props instead of twirling her way through the footlights? They hadn't been able to get together for Thanksgiving this year, so she hadn't mentioned the show to her mother yet. Still, anyone with half a brain would be able to figure out Amy would be staging this, her favorite ballet, to open her new studio.

And Connie Morgan had much more than half a brain, Amy thought as she speed-dialed Mom's number.

"Hello!" Mom answered, a little out of breath. "How's my girl today?"

"Fine. Are you on the treadmill?"

"Oh, you know how it is," she answered with a laugh.

"If I keep running, maybe old age won't be able to catch up with me."

Amy laughed in response, wishing for the umpteenth time that she'd inherited her mother's breezy attitude toward things in general. "I won't keep you, then. I just wanted to let you know we're putting on *The Nutcracker* on the eighteenth, here in Barrett's Mill."

She would have loved for Mom to attend, but not wanting to pressure her, she stopped short of putting that desire into words. The delighted gasp she got put her worries to rest.

"Your directing debut—of course I'll be there! I wouldn't miss it for the world. Then we can have a nice family Christmas with Helen and that big brother of mine."

More relieved than she'd anticipated, Amy relaxed enough to tease, "It's been a while. Do you remember how to get here?"

She humphed at that. "My new car has one of those fancy navigation systems."

"Sure, but do you know how to use it?"

"Such a comedian. Are you doing stand-up in your spare time now?"

"There's not much call for that down here." Amy chuckled. "Besides, that's the extent of my material. You gave me an opening the size of an 18-wheeler, and I took it."

"That's my girl, making the most of her opportunities," Mom praised her warmly. "It's so good to hear the old spunk back in your voice. It's been a long time coming."

That was a colossal understatement, but fortunately her break was over, so she didn't have time to brood about it. "I'm sorry to cut this short, but I have to get back to the kids now. See you soon."

"I'm looking forward to it. Love you, sweetie."

"Love you, too, Mom."

Ending the call, Amy sipped her water while studying the photos that chronicled her promising ballet career, which had been her only goal for as long as she could remember. When the kids started thundering back up the wooden steps and took their places onstage, her eyes drifted away from her past to focus on them.

Chattering to each other in hushed voices, they giggled while practicing the new steps she'd shown them earlier. With his soldiers trailing behind, Brad bounded up to take his spot, fresh enthusiasm glowing on his freckled face.

Apparently, the solution she'd come up with worked for him, she mused with a smile of her own as she went up the stairs to join her dancers for the second act. Maybe she was starting to get the hang of this teaching gig, after all.

"These look great, Fred," Jason commented while he assessed the older man's carpentry skills on some of the smaller set pieces. Not only had he finished cutting all of them out in detail, he'd painted them, too. His efforts would save Jason a ton of time. "I only dropped them off a couple days ago. How'd you get 'em done so fast?"

"Bored outta my mind," Fred grumped, but the smile on his face said he appreciated Jason's praise. "You can only watch so much of the History Channel."

"I hear that. I'd rather be doing something than watching TV any day. Has the doctor said when you can get back to work?"

The town's most talented mechanic groaned. "Another week, if I follow orders. 'Course, Helen won't let me do otherwise," he added with a mock glare over at his wife.

"You don't want to miss out on Christmas, do you?" she challenged with a glare of her own. "Especially with Amy here now and Connie coming in for a visit. We haven't all been together in years, and I'm not about to let you spoil it by being stubborn."

"Besides," Jason added with a grin, "with all the work you're putting in, you're gonna want to see *The Nutcracker*. It'd be a shame to have to make do with a recording when you could see it in person."

"Yeah, yeah. I get it. Just bring me some more to do," he pleaded. "I'm going bonkers cooped up here at the house."

"It's no picnic from where I'm sitting, either," his wife informed him testily.

They'd been married for longer than Jason had been alive, and he'd always been amused by their good-natured bickering. Done with fond smiles and a light touch, their back-and-forth was evidence of a solid relationship that had probably started before the two Barrett's Mill natives entered junior high.

They reminded him of his parents, who shared the kind of close, loving bond Jason longed for in his own life. Not long ago, he thought he'd found that with Rachel. He pictured himself settled in a home with a wife and kids, and when he'd asked her to be part of that, she'd quickly agreed. When she took off with another lumberjack and no explanation, Jason realized she'd told him only what she'd thought he wanted to hear.

Water under the bridge, he reminded himself, and

better left behind. They wanted different things, and now that he'd recovered from the sting of her rejection, he hoped she was happy.

"...not busy tomorrow night," Helen was saying, "I'd like to have you over for dinner, to thank you for all your help with the studio. I'll be making fried chicken."

Jason was pretty swamped these days, but he wasn't one to turn down a home-cooked meal. "I do like your fried chicken."

"That's settled, then. Just come by when you finish at the mill, and I'll have a place ready for you at the table."

"Sounds great. And I'll bring some more work for you," he promised Fred as he gathered up the pieces on his way to the door. "It sure is nice to have someone helping out who actually knows what they're doing."

"Connie's not all that mechanical, either," her uncle agreed with a chuckle. "Amy got that from her, I guess."

Jason had been wondering about Amy's father, and with that casual family comment it seemed the man was completely out of the picture. He knew how that went. He nearly mentioned that he'd also been pitching in to make repairs at the studio, then thought better of it. Hearing how much had slipped through the cracks while he was laid up wouldn't help Fred's recuperation at all, especially since the apartment in question was his niece's. Instead, Jason simply said good-night.

When he got to Arabesque, the parking spots in front of the studio were empty, so he took the one right in front of the door. The lobby was dark, but he noticed the lights over the stage were still on. Framed by the window, the elegant curtains drew his eyes to a single figure silhouetted in a spotlight.

It was Amy, clearly unaware that anyone was watching her. With her arms in a graceful pose, she seemed to glide over the floor, spinning slowly here and there, then pausing to write something on a piece of paper. When she tried a certain movement, even from a distance he saw her wince and grab her back with her hands.

His heart shot into his throat, and before he knew what he was doing, he was standing beside her. "Are you okay?"

"I'm fine," she all but snarled. "What are you doing out there spying on me?"

"Not spying," he corrected with a smile. "Admiring. Until you hurt your back, anyway. Before that, it was like watching a cloud move across the sky."

"It's nice of you to say that."

From her tone, he could tell she didn't share his opinion. He hadn't known her long, but she fascinated him, this delicate woman who had a vein of pure steel running through her. With a tough outer shell guarding a tender heart, she spoke to him in a way he'd never experienced before. In turn, he found himself wanting to protect her from harm and applaud her determination to take on the world single-handedly.

He didn't understand why, but there was definitely something special about Amy Morgan. Rather than argue with her, though, he opted to change the subject. "What're you doing?"

"Blocking steps for the kids." She showed him her notes, which featured a diagram labeled with things he couldn't begin to comprehend. "The original choreography is way too complicated for beginners, so I'm simplifying it for them. I'm designing a new dance for the prince and was trying it out when you came in."

"And interrupted you," he guessed with a sheepish grin. "Sorry. It looked good to me, though."

"I wish I could see for myself," she said wistfully. "I can't dance and watch at the same time."

"That fancy phone of yours must have a video function on it. You could record yourself."

Before he finished speaking, her face twisted with the kind of pain no one should have to endure. "I hate watching myself move," she ground out through clenched teeth. "It's ugly."

"Nothing about you is ugly," he assured her in his gentlest tone. "You're still the prettiest girl I've ever seen."

"That's sweet, but you don't have to lie to make me feel better."

Her eyes filled with equal parts gratitude and tears, and Jason scrambled to come up with some comforting words. "I'd never lie to a lady. My mom'd kill me."

"You're a grown man. How could she possibly find out?"

"Trust me, she'd know."

After a moment, Amy's wary look mellowed into a more friendly one, and she gave him a tentative smile. "In that case, you could help me with this. If you don't mind," she added hastily. "I know it's late."

Five a.m. would come pretty early, and he should have been in bed an hour ago, but her shy request drove any thoughts of sleep right out of his head. "I've got some time. Whattaya need me to do?"

Grasping his arms, Amy moved him into place and rattled off a series of moves. A dancer would be able to follow along, but a lumberjack? Not so much.

"Right," he responded with a laugh. "How 'bout in English?"

"Was I unclear?"

"Oh, I heard you fine. It's just I don't have a clue what you meant." Inspiration struck, and he suggested, "Maybe you could show me."

That got him a decidedly suspicious look. "Are you trying to get me to dance with you?" When he grinned, she rolled those beautiful eyes at him. "You're pathetically easy to read."

"I figure there's no sense in making a big mishmash of things." Opening his arms in his version of a ballet-style pose, he said, "Are we dancing or what?"

After a few seconds, she apparently decided he was harmless and ventured closer. He listened carefully to her instructions, and they slowly moved through the steps. Involved in one sport or another all his life, he'd managed not to embarrass himself at proms or his brothers' weddings. But next to Amy, he felt like a serious clod, and he reminded himself to be especially careful not to stomp on her toes.

Glancing down, he noticed how ridiculous their feet looked opposite each other. His shoes were not only huge, they were scuffed and stained—the opposite of her black patent flats with their classy velvet bows. The contrast was so complete, he couldn't help chuckling.

"What?" she asked, glancing around to see what was so funny.

"Our feet. They don't really go together, do they?"

She peeked at their shoes, then met his eyes with a laugh. "Not any more than the rest of us does. You're like a big redwood, and I'm a little twig."

"A beautiful twig," he amended with a warm smile. "One with gorgeous flowers that smell incredible."

She blushed, but to his surprise, she didn't look away. Instead, she held his gaze, searching his eyes for something. In that moment, he no longer cared that what he was feeling for her didn't make any sense. Whatever she was looking for, he wanted her to find it in him.

"It's jasmine," she said quietly, the corner of her mouth lifting invitingly. "Do you like it?"

"Very much." Sensing that he was approaching a line with her, he veered away before he crossed over it. Amy had been through an emotional wringer, and their growing friendship was fragile, at best. He wasn't about to destroy it by pushing things too fast. "'Course, I spend most of my time at the mill with machines that leak oil and guys that smell like... Well, you get the drift."

She laughed, a bright, carefree sound very much at odds with the serious woman he'd been getting acquainted with. It made him think of the young ballerina in the pictures on the wall, and he was pleased to discover that joyful girl still existed. Then and there, he decided he'd have to come up with some more ways to draw her out into the light. She deserved that, and odd as it was, it seemed he had a knack for doing it.

After a few minutes, she stopped directing his steps, shadowing him as he moved across the stage. They drifted from spotlight to spotlight, through the half-decorated ballroom to the huge tree with its flickering electric candles and old-fashioned ornaments. Since they weren't touching, it wasn't as if they were actually dancing together, but he felt a connection to her that went beyond the physical. He couldn't have explained it if he tried, but he liked the way it felt.

Pausing in front of the incomplete marble fireplace, he said, "I forgot to show you this."

Flipping a switch hidden behind the wall, he set the electric flames in motion. They reflected off the tinsel and sparkling balls, giving the set a warm, cozy glow.

"It's perfect," Amy breathed. She stared up at him, the Christmas lights twinkling in her eyes.

The urge to drop in for a kiss was nearly overpowering, and he sternly tamped it down. Amy trusted him, and he wanted to retain his good-guy status. "It's what you asked me for."

As sadness drifted through her expressive eyes, she frowned. "I don't always get what I ask for."

Laced with anguish, her comment drove through him like a knife. That this sweet, talented woman had been denied her life's dream struck him as the worst kind of tragedy. He pictured her alone in some hospital, begging for divine help that had never come. She'd picked herself up and moved on, but he could see part of her was stranded in the past, wishing for things that could never be. While he could imagine God redirecting her onto a different path for some reason, Jason knew that explanation would not only anger her, it might make her pull away from him. Whatever it took, he was determined not to let that happen.

"That's true for all of us. But you've made a new start here, and from where I'm standing, it looks like it's going really well."

"This isn't what I want," she confided in a desperate whisper. "I want to dance."

Suddenly, nothing meant more to him than to see her happy before he left. With that in mind, he said, "Then let's dance. Show me the routine you worked out for Clara and her prince."

As he took her hands in his, she stared at him as if she was seeing him for the first time. "Are you for real?"

"Yup. And I'm all yours." As soon as those words popped out, he realized how they sounded, and he cringed. "Sorry about that. I meant—"

"I know what you meant," she assured him, rewarding him with a grateful smile. "Thank you."

Being there felt so right, he'd have gladly stayed on that stage with her all night long. But he didn't think he should tell her that, so he went with an old standard. "You're welcome."

Chapter Five

"Is that what you're wearing?"

Jason stopped at the head of the stairs and turned to face the music. Olivia Barrett, his grandmother and authority on all things etiquette related, stood in the middle of the hallway, hands on her hips and a look of horror on her face.

"Yeah," he responded, trying not to laugh at what she clearly thought was a major fashion error. "Why?"

She let out an exasperated breath that spoke of decades of fighting with the Barrett men. "You look like you're going to a barn raising instead of dinner with the Morgans."

"It's Fred and Helen." Her odd expression set off alarm bells in his head, and he gave her a hard stare. "Right?"

She hesitated a few seconds, then said, "And Amy."

Groaning, he muttered, "What're you trying to do to me?"

Obviously embarrassed, she made a show of dusting something off the hand-carved newel post. Which of course was spotless. "Helen and I just want you kids to be happy."

Why did it not surprise him that Amy's aunt was in on this? Come to think of it, he should've figured out something was up when she asked him to dinner in the first place. Luring him in with fried chicken, no less.

Recognizing she and her friend meant well, he reassured Gram with a smile. "I'm very happy, being home and working at the mill. What makes you think I need more than that?"

From the glimmer in her eyes, Jason guessed the town gossip mill had ratted him out. "Brenda Lattimore saw you two at the studio last night. Dancing," she added in a triumphant voice.

"So? Amy's a dance teacher, and I was helping her put together some moves for her students." Even to his own ears, that sounded lame, and he couldn't help chuckling. "All right, you got me. I like her, okay?"

"We like her, too," Gram told him as they headed downstairs together. "She's a sweet girl who's taken a terrible blow. She needs all the understanding she can get."

"And you think I'm the one to give it to her, is that it?"

They'd reached the bottom of the stairs, and she turned to him with a look so full of love, he silently thanked God for making him part of her family. "Yes, I do. You've got a wonderful heart, just looking for the right woman to make a life with. Amy didn't land back in Barrett's Mill by accident, you know. God brought her here."

"For me," he said, filling in the blank for her. When she nodded, he shook his head. "I appreciate that, but before you and Helen start picking out wedding music, maybe we should find out what Amy thinks first."

"She'll love you, of course. All the girls do."

Which was the problem, complicated by the fact that Paul's assessment was dead-on: Jason was a sucker for a pretty face and a sad story. He fell too hard, too fast, and as he edged closer to twenty-five, he knew he couldn't keep on going that way. A guy could take only so much rejection, after all, and he'd promised himself the next time he proposed would be the last.

Since he hated to burst Gram's romantic bubble, he shook off his brooding with a chuckle. "How 'bout I go have dinner and then we'll see what happens after that?"

"But—"

"Let him go, Olivia," Granddad called out from the hospital bed that occupied their dining room. "You look fine, by the way. No matter what a woman says, a man looks better in his own plain clothes than someone else's fancy suit."

Jason had been living with them since returning to help out at the mill, but he still wasn't quite used to seeing the frail patient that had taken Granddad's place. At first, he could hardly stand to look at him, connected to an IV that fed him medicine to ease the pain of the cancer destroying his body. Gradually, the man's upbeat attitude, driven by a belief that his life had gone according to divine plan, eased some of Jason's sadness.

But this Christmas would be his last. The whole family knew it, and Will and Olivia refused to avoid the topic, instead choosing to keep it in the open and treasure every day they had together. Jason and Paul had come back from Oregon to fulfill Granddad's wish for reopening the mill to produce furniture again. That he'd lived long enough to enjoy their success was something Jason thanked God for every night before he went to sleep.

When Jason realized his grandparents were staring at him, he put aside his dark thoughts and summoned a smile. "Well, I'm off. I've got my cell phone if you need me."

"I don't suppose you'd bring me some of Helen's fried chicken?" Granddad asked hopefully. "Hers is almost as good as Olivia's."

"You got it." Jason waved as he opened the door. Kissing his grandmother's cheek, he said, "'Night, Gram."

"Good night, little bear," she replied, using the nickname she'd given him as a child. "Mind your manners, now."

Knowing she'd hear all about his behavior from Helen long before he made it home, he couldn't help laughing. "Yes, ma'am."

"Everyone will be here Sunday after church to decorate the house," she reminded him through the screen door. "Amy's got quite the eye for Christmas decorations, from what I hear. Maybe you can get some suggestions from her."

A blind man could see where she was headed with that one, and he teased, "It'd be easier to just invite her over to help."

"If you want," she said, as if the possibility hadn't even crossed her mind. Her expression mirrored the one Helen had given him yesterday, and he trotted down the steps shaking his head.

If she got her way, he and Amy would be hitched by Valentine's Day. Given his less-than-stellar track record, the mere thought of that should've chilled the blood in his veins. But it didn't. That meant one of two things, he mused as he went down the driveway and turned onto the sidewalk. Either the idea was so ridiculous he'd already dismissed it, or he liked it. Whichever one was correct, he had the feeling his nice, quiet life was about to get a lot more complicated.

As he strolled toward the Morgan place, it occurred to him that the stick-to-the-plan ballet teacher probably wasn't the type who'd be thrilled about having a surprise guest for dinner. Taking his phone from the pocket of his good jeans, he thumbed through his contacts list to the number she'd given him when he signed on to tackle the sets for her show.

"Jason? Is something wrong?"

"Nah, just calling to warn you I'm coming for dinner tonight. Your aunt made it sound like payback for helping at the studio, but Gram let it slip that they're trying to get us together."

She'd called herself a perfectionist, and he assumed she'd be irritated by the unexpected change in plans. Instead, she laughed. "That explains the good china and five-layer chocolate cake in the kitchen."

"Aw, man. You mean the one with her secret raspberry sauce and fresh raspberries?"

"That's the one."

"No one can resist that cake," he said. "It tied for first place at the county fair last year."

"With what?"

"My gram's cranberry cobbler," he replied proudly. "You should try it sometime."

After a moment, she asked, "Are you asking me over for dessert some night?"

Was he? He hadn't intended to, but now that he replayed his comment in his head, he could see how she'd get that impression. He was normally much smoother than that around women, and this one was on the other end of the phone, so he had no excuse for the slipup. What was wrong with him, anyway?

Then he recalled Gram's invitation, and as he entered the Morgans' driveway, he decided to go for it. "Sure. How 'bout Sunday?"

She was standing on the front porch, and she waved to him as she said, "That would be nice. What time?"

Closing his phone, Jason took the steps two at a time and greeted her with a smile. "Does lunchtime work for you?"

"Sure."

"I should warn you, we'll be decorating the house that day, so the whole family will be there. It might get a little zooey, but the upside is there'll be lots of good food and Christmas music."

"I like both those things," she commented with a shy smile that made his heart roll over in his chest. "Thanks for inviting me."

"No problem."

He opened the door for her to go inside, and she turned to him with a frown. "Aunt Helen told me your grandfather's not doing well. I'm so sorry."

"We all are."

With eyes full of sympathy, she touched his arm in a comforting gesture. "If there's anything I can do to help, please let me know."

Pushing aside a sudden wave of sadness, he forced a grin. "Coming over and pretending you don't mind being set up with me will do fine."

"I can manage that."

Smiling, she moved past him and went inside. The scent of fried chicken and fresh corn reached him where he was standing in the living room, and he poked his head through the doorway. "Helen, that smells amazing."

"You haven't seen anything yet."

"I heard something about chocolate and raspberries."

"You heard right," she assured him. "For now, could you run out and tell Fred dinner's ready? He's tinkering out in the shop and can't hear me over that saw."

"I heard you," Fred grumbled from the back door. "I was waiting for Jason 'cause I knew you wouldn't be putting anything on the table till he got here."

Southern hospitality, Jason thought with a grin. He sure had missed it during the five years he'd been wandering around the country. Once they were all seated at the table, Helen brought in a platter heaped with crisp, golden-fried chicken that made his stomach rumble in anticipation. "Sorry about that. I worked through lunch today."

"So, things are busy out at the mill?" Fred asked as he passed dishes along.

"Crazy busy, but we're all glad for the work."

"Carpentry isn't as exciting as lumberjacking, I'd imagine."

"True," Jason responded, "but I'm not liable to break my neck doing it, either. Besides, I like being home, especially during the holidays. I used to race back for Christmas and leave right after. This year, I won't be doing that."

"That means you'll be around for the Starlight Festival," Helen said while she spooned fluffy mashed potatoes onto his plate. "When's the last time you went to that?"

"It's been a while," he admitted.

"I vaguely remember that," Amy said, punctuating the comment with her fork. "There's all kinds of goodies, and white lights strung all over the place like stars. Then they light up the tree in the square."

Her eyes shimmered with excitement, and he was pleased to get a glimpse of the joy he kept hoping to see in her. It made him wonder if the little girl she'd once been was still in there somewhere, waiting for a chance to come out and play again.

"The whole town turns out for it," Fred told her. "Local business owners donate the food, and it gives us all a chance to get together to celebrate the holidays."

The conversation died down while they worked their way through Helen's excellent meal. When she brought the promised cake and coffee to the table, she said, "Amy, I was just thinking the festival might be a nice way to let more people know about Arabesque. I could help you put something together, if you want."

Amy's expression dimmed, and she sighed. "I'd love to, Auntie, but we're just scraping by as it is. If enrollment doesn't pick up, I'm not sure we're going to make it until spring."

Jason was well acquainted with the tough business climate around Barrett's Mill these days. Reopening the mill had been a godsend for the local craftsmen they'd been able to bring on. He just wished they could afford to hire more of them. Expanding the crew would not only make less work for each pair of hands, it would give some talented people a welcome influx of cash.

While the delicious cake fell apart in his mouth, an

idea popped into his head, and he quickly swallowed. "How 'bout if you advertise the show at the Starlight Festival?"

"There's no marketing allowed," Helen reminded him. "It's supposed to be a fun, free event."

"Sure, but if you offered a treat free of charge, you could wrap it in something *Nutcracker*-ish with the studio's logo on it, right?"

Amy's eyes lit up, and she leaned forward with sudden interest. "What did you have in mind?"

Turning to Helen, he grinned. "Your pralines. They're made with nuts, so they tie in with the show. And they're delicious, besides. It's a win-win."

"That's a great idea, Jason." Amy turned hopeful eyes on her aunt. "If you make them, I'll take care of the wrapping and handing out."

"Count me in," Jason added. "It'll be fun."

Faced with the two of them, Helen tipped her head with an indulgent smile. "I suppose I could whip up a batch or two. But where will you find *Nutcracker* wrappers?"

"Online," Amy answered immediately. "I'll get them overnighted so we have them in time. We'll wrap them up Saturday morning right before the tree lighting. It'll be perfect," she added, beaming across the table at Jason.

"Yeah, it will." Returning that smile was the easiest thing he'd ever done, and he ignored the annoying voice in the back of his mind cautioning him that he was headed onto very thin ice. Even if that ended up being true, his gut was telling him trouble with Amy would be well worth it.

* * *

The Barrett's Mill Starlight Festival definitely lived up to its name.

The night was brisk, but nothing compared to the winters she'd spent in New York City. The clear sky was filled with stars that rivaled the twinkle lights strung through the oaks and elms in the square. In the middle of it all, standing regally above the fray, towered a blue spruce comparable to any she'd seen outside of Rockefeller Center. Draped in strands of lights, it was dark, waiting for the lighting ceremony later in the evening.

"See the star up there?" Jason asked, pointing to it. "Granddad's father made that for the first time the town decorated the tree."

"What a nice tradition," Amy commented as her eyes traveled up to it. "They probably didn't need a cherry picker to put it up back then."

"Yeah, they conned some poor sap into scaling the trunk and wiring it in place." Chuckling, he shook his head. "Can you imagine how sticky he'd be with pine pitch all over him? Stuff must've stuck to him for a week."

Amy hadn't considered that, and she marveled at the practical way his mind worked. She was a creative person by nature, and her involvement pretty much ended at the concept stage. In the short time she'd known him, Jason had proven himself adept at making her fanciful designs work in three dimensions. Piece by piece, together they were bringing her vision for *The Nutcracker* to life. Theirs was an unusual collaboration, to be sure, but so far it seemed to be working.

Hefting the large basket of pralines, he scanned the

crowd from his much higher vantage point. "Okay. Where did you wanna start?"

"You know, I'm perfectly capable of carrying that myself," she protested.

"Not as long as I'm here."

She bristled at that. "Excuse me?"

He seemed to realize he'd insulted her, and he deflected her temper with a soothing grin. "That didn't come out right. I meant I'm happy to help a lady out by hauling a basket around the square for her. Since these are your aunt's treats, I'm figuring it'll lighten up quick enough."

As if to prove his point, a middle-aged couple approached them with bright smiles. They looked vaguely familiar, but Amy couldn't quite place them until the man began talking.

"Good evening, you two." While his greeting was for them both, he added a fatherly nod for her. "It's wonderful to see you again, Amy. It's been a while, so I'm not sure you remember me."

"Pastor Griggs," she said, a sinking feeling in the pit of her stomach. It only worsened when she glanced at his wife, and she struggled to keep her composure. In her mind, they represented everything she'd turned her back on, and running into them tonight was awkward, at best. "Mrs. Griggs. How are you tonight?"

"Busy as always during the holiday season," the woman replied in the gentle voice that had taught her the Sunday-school lessons she'd adored. The ones where she'd learned that God loved and watched over all His children. She'd believed that for a long time, until harsh experience had taught her otherwise. The day He abandoned her was the beginning of the worst time in her life.

It was bad enough the rest of the year, but Christmas was especially hard for her. While everyone else was full of grace and good cheer, she mourned what she'd lost out on that dark, icy road, knowing it was gone forever.

Jason was calmly chatting with them as if nothing was amiss, even though he'd confided to her how sad he was about his grandfather. She found herself envying his levelheaded perspective, and she made an attempt to copy his behavior. Smiling and nodding, she did her best to participate in the lighthearted conversation, and to her surprise, her dark mood began to brighten.

Until the pastor said, "I'm sure you're very busy with the studio, Amy, but we'd love to have you back at the Crossroads Church. Our little family hasn't been quite the same without you."

Amy saw absolutely no reason to worship a God who'd turned His back on her, and she swallowed hard to keep from blurting out her true feelings. "Thank you for the invitation."

Apparently, Mrs. Griggs sensed her attitude and changed tracks with a laugh. "Don't be fooled, dear. What he's really after is another soprano for the choir. We've lost a few and are hunting for some to replace them."

"No one's sick, I hope," Amy said.

"One of the ladies has a baby due on Christmas Eve, and she won't be able to sing. Another moved unexpectedly when her husband got a new job out of state, and the others—" She shrugged. "You know how it is."

"You have such a lovely voice, though," her husband chimed in with an optimistic look. "I'm sure your singing would be wonderful."

He'd nailed her weakness, Amy groaned silently. Despite her ongoing battle with the Almighty, she loved Christmas music for its upbeat, joyful content. Peace on earth, goodwill toward everyone—even a lapsed Christian like her could appreciate such hopeful messages.

But agreeing to sing would make her the worst kind of hypocrite, and she wouldn't be able to live with herself. "I'm afraid I'm not active in the church anymore. Much as I'd like to help out, it wouldn't feel right to do that when I don't attend services."

The Griggses exchanged a look that told her they already knew what she'd just told them, and the pastor's wife patted her shoulder in a comforting gesture. "We completely understand, dear, and we're not trying to coerce you into doing something you're not comfortable with. If you'd like to join us, we'd be happy to have you."

Amy couldn't believe she'd heard the woman correctly. "You mean, I can join the choir but not come to church?"

"Yes," the pastor replied without hesitation. "No one will pressure you for more than you want to do. You have my word on that."

At first, his promise made no sense to her at all. Then it occurred to her he was probably thinking she'd change her mind once she got reacquainted with the people in the congregation. Maybe he was right, she acknowledged, maybe not. But she couldn't deny that celebrating Christmas in her hometown held a nostalgic appeal for her.

She glanced up at Jason, who met her questioning look with a grin. "Most of us can't sing a lick, but it's a lotta fun."

"You're in the church choir?" she asked, well and truly amazed.

"Sure. It's a great place to meet girls."

His wicked grin made her laugh, and she had to admit that knowing he'd be there was a plus for her. She'd been on her own for so long, wishing she could find a way to belong to a community somewhere. Here was a golden opportunity, staring her in the face. All she had to do was go into the church for rehearsals, she reasoned. How hard could it be?

"Your cousin Brenda has the music," the preacher nudged gently. "I'm sure she'd copy it for you, and then you could decide after that. If you're interested, we rehearse on Tuesday nights, from six to eight."

"I'll definitely think about it."

They each took a praline, agreeing to spread the word about her upcoming production. As they headed off to circulate, she wondered at the turn her evening had taken. If they'd asked her about the choir an hour ago, she'd have politely but firmly refused. Now, for some reason, she was more open to it. Could it be the town's undeniable Christmas spirit was rubbing off on her? Anything was possible, she supposed.

"Punch?" Jason asked, nodding toward the table loaded down with huge punch bowls and paper cups.

"Please."

She took the basket from him, fully intending to keep it. But when he returned with their drinks, he smoothly retrieved it from her. While they resumed their aimless course through the square, she said, "You're a very stubborn man."

That got her a bright grin. "Yeah."

"Jenna complains about your brother Paul being the same way. It must run in your family."

His expression dimmed, and in his eyes she noticed something she hadn't yet seen: anxiety. He'd been so kind to her, she felt awful for upsetting him, even though it was an accident. "I'm sorry, Jason. Did I say something wrong?"

"No, it's just—" Taking her elbow, he guided her to a quieter spot in a stand of trees away from the crowd. "There's something you need to know about me."

It sounded so ominous, she felt her pulse ratchet up several notches. Did she want to know? she wondered. She'd learned to keep people—especially men—at a safe distance to avoid being hurt. But now, she was touched that he valued their friendship enough to share an important secret with her. Because he trusted her, she felt more confident about trusting him in return. "Okay. Go ahead."

After a heavy sigh, he fixed her with an intense gaze she'd never seen from him. "Paul and I aren't related."

"I don't understand. You and everyone else in town told me you're brothers."

"We are, but not the usual way. His mom, Diane, works with kids at teen centers she runs here and in Cambridge, which is where she met my mother twenty-five years ago. She and Tom adopted me from her before I was born."

Amy's jaw fell open in shock, and she frantically searched for a logical reaction to his stunning news. "Who is she?"

"I have no idea. That was part of the deal they made, and my parents have stood by their word."

"But didn't you wonder about her while you were

growing up?" Amy pressed in a whisper. "I mean, she was your mother."

"She wasn't ready for me when I came along," he explained in a tone much calmer than hers. "She gave me a chance to have a better life, and whoever she is, I'll always be grateful to her for that."

"I'd be furious," Amy hissed at the selfish woman she'd never meet. How could a mother surrender her newborn child? Unmarried and alone at what she assumed was a similar age, her own mother had never even considered such a thing.

Jason took her anger in stride, easing her temper with a smile. "Your mom took on the world for you and made it work. Not everyone is that strong."

Since he'd come to terms with the situation, Amy concluded that it was ridiculous for her to debate a teenager's decision with him. Shaking off her lingering resentment, she did her best to return the smile. "I guess you're right about that. Dad left when I was a baby, but Mom never let him being gone affect me. She's pretty amazing."

"You must've gotten that from her." Holding up his cup, he tapped hers in a toast. "To Christmas in Barrett's Mill. Welcome home, Amy."

She'd heard grander speeches, but none had warmed her withered heart the way his simple toast did. There was something about this towering lumberjack with the kind eyes that made her want to start dreaming of better things to come. "Welcome home, Jason. Merry Christmas."

He polished off his punch in one swallow and tossed his cup into a nearby bin. Then he rubbed his hands together and picked up the basket again. "Enough serious talk. Let's give out the rest of these so we can enjoy ourselves."

"Sounds good."

With his height and outgoing personality, it didn't take long for them to empty the basket. Several people asked about the studio and what kinds of classes she'd be offering after the holidays. Fortunately, Amy had the foresight to bring along business cards, and by the time they'd finished their circuit of the square, all the cards and candies were gone.

"This is fabulous," she approved. "If even half those folks bring their kids in after New Year's, I'll have enough students for another beginning ballet class."

Jason gave her an admiring look. "Y'know, I snuck in the other day while you were teaching that bunch of six-year-olds. You're great with them, and the way they stare up at you is really cute."

"I like kids in general, but that group is so great, I think I have even more fun than they do."

"It shows. You're gonna make a fantastic mom someday."

His comment plucked a sensitive chord deep inside her, and she tried to accept his compliment the way she knew she should. Swallowing hard, she managed to thank him in a more or less normal voice.

Unfortunately, he was more perceptive than she'd anticipated, and his face clouded with concern. "Did I say something wrong?"

"No, it's nothing. Sorry," she added lamely. "It's been a big day, and I'm a little tired, I guess."

"It's not nothing, but if you don't wanna talk about it, that's fine. I understand."

Meeting his eyes, she found nothing but compassion

in them. As a rule, she kept her private issues to herself, not wanting to discuss painful things with people who couldn't possibly relate to them. Jason was different, though. He'd trusted her with something very personal about himself, and she knew if she confided in him, he'd be sympathetic.

So, after a deep breath, she nutshelled it for him. "I can't have children."

"Because of the accident?" When she nodded, his rugged face twisted with sympathy. "Amy, I'm so sorry. Are you sure there's no way around it?"

"The surgeries I went through made sure of that. It was the main reason my fiancé left," she heard herself add. She hadn't meant to share that detail, but since it was out in the open, she decided to clear it all out of her system. "Having a family was really important to him, and he refused to consider adoption."

"Love is what makes a family," Jason said tersely. "If he was too narrow-minded to see that, you're better off without him."

The utter conviction in his tone drove off some of her sadness, and she rewarded his thoughtfulness with her biggest, brightest smile. "Thank you for saying that. It was very sweet."

He gave her a slow, very male grin. "That's me."

"The girls around here must fall all over you." The grin widened mischievously, and she couldn't help laughing. "Just so you know, I won't be joining them."

"Really?" The gold in his eyes sparked with curiosity, and he moved a half step closer. "Why?"

It was a moronically simple question, but while his gaze seemed to warm the chilly evening air, her brain went completely blank. He was so down-to-earth, with his easygoing demeanor and generous nature. Here, in her tiny hometown of all places, she'd found someone who accepted her just as she was, flaws and all. Being female, she couldn't help being drawn to him and his bright optimism, but at the same time she resisted getting any closer. The question, as he'd so directly put it, was why.

While she hunted for a decent response, he flashed her a confident grin. "That's fine. But fair warning— I'm gonna change your mind."

His smug tone irked her, and she snorted derisively. "Not hardly."

"Better watch yourself," he teased. "That Blue Ridge accent's starting to come back."

Relieved to switch to a less volatile topic, she griped, "It's hard not to talk that way when everyone around you does."

"Don't get your back up. I like it."

With that, he sauntered on ahead of her, swinging the empty basket and whistling along with the rendition of "Rockin' Around the Christmas Tree" playing on the loudspeakers. As she hurried to catch up with his long strides, she wondered who he thought he was, speaking to her that way. The fact that he could potentially be right had nothing to do with her current frame of mind, of course. It was just one more reason to keep a safe distance between them.

The trouble was, the time she spent with Jason was the happiest she'd ever been away from the stage. She wasn't a face-fanning romantic, but even she recognized that her desire to be with him meant something. Something that could derail everything if she lost sight of her goal to reclaim her independence and take control of her life again.

She simply couldn't allow that to happen, she reminded herself sternly as she joined the crowd milling around the tree. Because her instincts were warning her that if she lost herself in Jason Barrett, she might never find her way out.

Chapter Six

Who on earth was knocking on her door?

Slitting her eyes open just enough to see the clock on her bedside table, Amy groaned. Eight o'clock on a Sunday morning was sleeping time, not answering-the-door time. But the noise persisted, and she dragged herself from her comfy nest and peeked out the window to see who had the gall to interrupt her only day off this way.

"Come on, Ames," Brenda said in a voice far too chipper for the hour. "I see you in there."

Stubbornly refusing to give in, she grumbled, "I'm sleeping. What do you want?"

"I've got your choir music."

Home delivery, she mused with a yawn. How convenient. "Fine. Shove it under the door."

She heard crinkling, then a quiet laugh. "I can't now that Jason installed that door sweep. Quit being difficult and open up."

Since she apparently had no choice, Amy reluctantly turned the dead bolt and let her cousin inside. Dressed in her churchgoing best, her makeup impeccable and not a hair out of place, Brenda swept her with a practiced glance. "You're a mess. You can't go to church looking like that."

"I wasn't planning to," Amy informed her through another yawn, "or anywhere else, until I go to the Barretts' decorating party at noon."

"Let me get this straight." Her unwanted visitor plopped down in one of the two kitchen chairs and fixed her with a puzzled look. "You're going to sing in the Crossroads choir but not go to services?"

"Of course not." When Brenda tilted her head in confusion, she amended her quick answer. "Well, probably not, even though Pastor Griggs said I could. It's just that he caught me off guard at the Starlight Festival when he asked me to help out. Have you ever tried to say no to that man?"

"I see your point." She smiled, but it faded almost right away. "You know, it might be good for you to come this morning. I know it's been a while, but I think—"

"It's been a while for a very good reason," Amy reminded her curtly.

Brenda pressed her glossy lips together, as if she was choosing her words carefully. It wasn't like her to be so cautious, so she must be winding up for a doozy. "I'm getting a crick in my neck. Could you sit down for a minute?"

Never a good sign, but Amy did as she asked. When they were eye to eye, her cousin went on. "I know we all agreed never to talk about your accident, but there's something I've been wanting to tell you, and you need to listen until I'm done."

Because she adored her bubbly cousin, Amy braced herself for an unpleasant conversation and nodded. "Go ahead."

"I saw the pictures of your car," she began in a hushed tone. Slowly shaking her head, she went on. "This is hard for me to say, but I couldn't believe they pulled you out of that wreck alive. The cops and firemen said as much when your mom met them at the hospital."

"Really? She never said anything to me."

"No one wanted to upset you," Brenda explained, patting her hand in a consoling gesture. "We were so grateful to still have you with us, nothing else mattered."

"That was two years ago. Why are you bringing this up now?"

Brenda took a deep breath and fixed her with a somber look. "God didn't abandon you, Amy. He saved you. Back then, you ate, slept and breathed ballet. You might have been successful, but you never seemed very happy to me."

"I was engaged, if you'll recall."

"Sure, to a man who bailed when things got tough. If you ask me, Devon's the one you should be punishing, not God."

"I didn't ask you." The words may have sounded tough, but even Amy heard the uncertainty in her voice. The truth was, Brenda had touched on a very sensitive spot, and to make matters worse, she was probably right.

"No, you didn't, but that's never stopped me before." Setting the sheet music on the table, she stood and pushed the chair back in. "I won't mention church again, but I'll be saving a seat for you if you change your mind. Unless you'd rather sit with Jason," she added with a knowing look.

"Oh, please!" Amy moaned. "Not you, too. Which reminds me—thanks so much for spreading it all around town that we were dancing at the studio the other night. Folks can't stop talking about it."

"Because it's so cute," Brenda cooed. "He's this hunky lumberjack, and you're this tiny dancer, and it was just precious seeing you together that way."

Even though he wasn't there, Amy could hear Jason laughing at the dreamy description of them, and she couldn't keep back a smile. "Was it?"

"Absolutely. If you have any sense at all, you'll hold on to that one. He's as solid as they come, and more loyal than an old hound."

"If he's so great, how come he's not serious with anyone?"

"I heard something about an ex-fiancée who stole his truck and broke his heart," Brenda answered with a smirk. "Sound familiar?"

"Yeah," Amy admitted slowly. "Except for the truck thing."

Laughing, Brenda gave her a quick hug. "I hope we'll see you later. If not, enjoy your day with the Barretts."

Once her chatty cousin had left, Amy tried to get back to sleep. But something Brenda had said kept echoing in her mind.

If you ask me, Devon's the one you should be punishing, not God.

She had a point, Amy reluctantly acknowledged. While the accident had been the first blow, Devon's betrayal had been the one that truly took her feet out from under her. That realization cleared her perception of what had happened, and she sat up in bed as the epiphany took hold. It wasn't as if she was handicapped, confined to a wheelchair or a bed. Using her connections, she could easily have gotten an administrative job with any dance company, and they could have adopted children to create the family they'd both longed for.

That was what Jason would have done. She believed that with a certainty that was more than a little frightening. They'd just met, and already she had more faith in him than she'd ever had in her fiancé. Was it Jason, with his grounded upbringing and generous heart? Or was it her, someone who'd made it through the fire and come out the other side with a fresh perspective? Instinct told her it was a combination of the two, and for the first time since her accident, she listened to that small voice in the back of her mind.

Feeling more energetic than she did most mornings, she flung back the covers and quickly got ready to leave. She chose a simple dress and shoes appropriate for church in a small town. Poking her nose outside, she decided a sweater would be smart, and she backtracked to get one from her closet.

The Crossroads Church stood at the head of Main Street, so she decided to walk. As she made her way toward the quaint country chapel, she noticed several families doing the same. They were all ahead of her on the sidewalk, chatting and laughing together. The town's two other churches were nearby, and people veered off to enter one or the other, waving to their neighbors as they parted ways. It was a familiar scene from her childhood that made her smile.

When she was alone on the sidewalk, though, doubt started creeping in. Logic told her she was headed to a building, nothing more. But the little girl who still lived inside her knew better. God was well aware that she'd shunned Him, and while she was convinced she was doing the right thing, she dreaded going into His house to ask His forgiveness.

Her feet began dragging, and as she approached the walkway leading to the front steps, she'd all but stopped moving. There was a small crowd out front, greeting each other before heading inside for the service. The sight of them stopped her cold, and she silently berated her cousin for talking her into coming. This was the last time she'd listen to Brenda, Amy vowed as she started to walk away.

"Amy?"

When she turned back, she was surprised to find Jason trotting down the steps to meet her halfway.

"Hey there," he said easily. "How're you this morning?"

"Fine. What are you doing out here?"

"Looking for you."

She rolled her eyes. "Did Brenda tell you to do that?"

"Nope. Thought of it all on my own." The sunlight warmed the gold in his eyes, and they crinkled as he smiled. "After what the pastor said last night, I was hoping you'd come."

"I wasn't going to, but Brenda came by this morning and got me thinking."

"About?"

How could she explain it to him when she didn't quite understand it herself? Sifting through her thoughts, she came up with something he might be able to grasp. "I've been punishing God for what happened to me, but what hurt the most was Devon leaving. He could have stuck it out, but he didn't. Looking back, there were other times he gave up when things got difficult. I just didn't see it that way at the time."

"So, if the accident hadn't ruined things between you, it would've been something else later on."

His clear view of her failed relationship nudged her that last step to admitting the truth she hadn't been able to put into words until now. "Exactly. With his wimpy attitude, sooner or later our marriage probably would've failed anyway."

He didn't touch her, but his admiring look felt like a gentle caress. "Not everyone is as strong as you."

No one had ever referred to her that way, and she blinked in astonishment. "You think I'm strong?"

"Very. Look at what you've overcome to get to where you are. Strength isn't always like this." To demonstrate, he made a fist. "Sometimes it's like this." Opening his hand, he went on. "When we put aside our own problems and reach out to help someone else. We all have that kind of power. We just have to make the choice to use it to make the world around us better."

"I guess I can leave now," Amy told him with a grin. "Even Pastor Griggs couldn't come up with anything better than that."

"You never know. He might surprise you."

The church bells started ringing, calling people in to worship, and he began walking toward the steps that had intimidated her into stopping. Confused that he apparently meant to go inside without her, she asked, "You're leaving?"

Half turning, he said, "If you're interested, I'll be sitting in the back pew on the left."

"Aren't you going to try to talk me into going with you?"

"Granddad taught me you can't convince someone to do something they're dead set against," he replied with a smile. "But if you change your mind, you're welcome to join me."

His faith was obviously very important to him, and the fact that he'd never attempted to coerce her into following his example told her just how open-minded he was. Since her accident, well-meaning people all around her had told her what to do, when and how much. She'd lost control of her own life, and that had made her resistant to advice in general.

Jason respected her wishes, even if they conflicted with his own. As he disappeared into the vestibule, she waited a few seconds, debating with herself. Finally, she decided she was being ridiculous and trailed after him.

The service was about to begin, and the small sanctuary was filled to capacity. Tall stained-glass windows lined both walls, throwing prisms of light onto the old floorboards. Judy Griggs noticed her from the choir risers and sent her a delighted smile. Returning the gesture, Amy recalled a Christmas pageant when the pastor's wife had graciously allowed her to lead the angels down the aisle, twirling and leaping her way toward the manger set up in front of the altar.

When she was a budding dancer, it had been a dream come true for her. Thinking of it now reminded her that no matter what had gone on in her life since then, she'd once belonged here. God had houses all over the world, but she suspected that if she'd gone into any of them, she wouldn't have felt the same as she did this morning. But in this place, filled with such wonderful memories, she felt at home. That wasn't a coincidence, she knew, and it made her feel more confident about her decision to venture inside.

Just like he'd promised, she found Jason sitting on

the far left side, with an empty space beside him on the pew. When she approached, he gave her an encouraging smile and patted the seat he'd saved for her. She sat, and then noticed that Paul and Chelsea were sitting much farther up with a large group of people she recognized as the Barrett clan.

"Don't you want to sit with your family?" she whispered to Jason.

"Maybe next time. Today, I thought it'd be better if you could make a quiet exit."

He'd chosen this spot to make her more comfortable, she realized. His thoughtfulness amazed her, and she rewarded him with a grateful smile. "I should be fine, but I appreciate you thinking of it. Thank you."

"You're welcome." As the organist began playing, he offered Amy a hymnal. "Mostly, I'm dying to hear how well you sing."

"Not that well," she confessed as they stood. "I'm hoping the choir is big enough no one will notice."

While the congregation started singing "Rock of Ages," his face lit up with enthusiasm. "You're gonna join the Christmas choir?"

Actually, she hadn't made up her mind until just now, but his reaction was all the proof she needed that it was the right choice. Nodding, she picked up the verse in midphrase to avoid annoying the people around them. Jason didn't seem worried about that, though, and he leaned in to murmur, "I have to tell you, I'm real glad you're here."

Taking her eyes from the page, she looked up at him and smiled. Because that was precisely how she felt about it herself, and she recognized that was mostly because of him. He hadn't allowed her to turn tail and run, but he hadn't dragged her into the chapel, either.

In his calm, steady way, he'd encouraged her to take this step while allowing her to choose for herself. Because that was the kind of person he was.

Finding him at this point in her life was just what she needed. Singing words that had been written generations ago, she silently thanked God for bringing her back to where she belonged.

"Gram, Granddad," Jason said proudly, "this is Amy Morgan. Amy, these are my grandparents, Olivia and Will."

"Come in, come in!" Gram exclaimed, embracing Amy with enthusiasm. "We've known your aunt and uncle forever, and Jason's told us wonderful things about you. We're thrilled to finally meet you."

"Thanks so much for inviting me today," she said quietly. "I know this is a family gathering, and it was nice of you to include me."

"Always room for more," Granddad assured her. "It's a big house."

So far, so good, Jason thought. Amy was a little tense, but he hoped she'd relax once she met everyone and figured out how to keep them all straight. "It smells great in here."

"Roast beef and gingerbread," his grandfather announced eagerly. "I've been smelling it all morning, and I'm starving. Maybe you and Amy can go in and hurry them along."

"Gotcha."

Ushering Amy through the archway, he paused to let her get her bearings before wading into the bustling crew in his grandmother's kitchen. Mom was just taking a batch of gingerbread men out of the oven to add to the ones already cooling on a large rack. When she caught sight of him with their guest, she set the hot tray down and hurried over.

"There's my bear," she cooed, beaming up at him before turning her attention to the petite woman who seemed to be doing her best to hide behind him. Laughing, Mom grasped her hand and drew her forward. "And you must be Amy. I'm Diane Barrett. Welcome to chaos."

"Thank you for having me," she replied so quietly Jason could barely hear her. It struck him as odd that she'd be so timid around new people after all those years performing. Then again, in those days she'd been elevated on a stage, a good distance from the audience. Close-up contact was a whole different ball game. While he was mulling that over, she surprised him again.

"Is there anything I can do to help?" she asked, a bit more loudly this time.

"We're covered in here, but I think Paul and Chelsea could use a hand in the living room. We've got a ten-foot tree and a dozen totes filled with ornaments that need new hooks. Last year, somebody—" she glared across the kitchen at Jason's father "—tossed out all the old ones."

"They were rusty or bent, or both," he said defensively while he sharpened a carving knife.

Sensing an ongoing argument, Jason laughed. "Let me guess. You forgot to buy new ones."

"No, I bought a bunch after Christmas last year. I just forgot where I put them."

"Paul stopped to pick some up after church, and now

he and Chelsea are stuck in the living room string-ing ornaments," Mom said. "I'm sure they'd appreci-ate your help."

"It beats checking the lights," Jason commented, giv-ing Amy a questioning look. "Wanna help?"

"Okay." Staying glued to his side, she murmured, "How many people are here, anyway?"

After a quick calculation, he came up with sixteen. Her eyes nearly bugged out of her head, and he chuck-led. "Is that a lot?"

"For your immediate family, yes. Then again, it's usually just my mom and me, so I'm not the best judge." Outside the living room, she tugged him to a stop. "I've met Paul and Chelsea, but before we go in, can you point out the others for me so I can keep everyone straight?"

"Sure."

As he went through the gathering of brothers, wives and children, she watched carefully, and he assumed she was committing their faces to memory. When he took her around the room for introductions, she seemed more confident than she had earlier, and he marveled at the change in her demeanor when she was prepared. Since he was a by-the-seat-of-his-pants kind of guy, it hadn't occurred to him she might need a briefing on his large family before being tossed into the fray.

Obviously, this was one lady who preferred to test the water before she jumped in. Lesson learned, he mused with a grin.

"Amy, I'm so glad to see you," Chelsea gushed from her seat on a hassock in front of a decorations bin. "Paul is no help at all."

"It's not my fault," he protested. "Those hooks are too small."

"They're normal-size hooks," his wife informed him curtly. "It's your hands that are too big."

"My hands are pretty small, so I'll help with these," Amy offered. "That way the guys can do the lights."

When Jason caught sight of the knotted balls of cords and bulbs, he groaned. "I thought we coiled 'em up nice and neat last year."

"We did," Paul confirmed, "but they didn't stay that way. We've gotta come up with something else for next time."

"We should wrap them around some of those empty wire spools we've got at the mill," Jason suggested. "They're just taking up space in the storage room."

"Great idea," Chelsea said approvingly. "You're elected to take care of that."

"Huh. That'll teach me to keep my big mouth shut."

Amy laughed at that, and he congratulated himself on making her feel more at ease in what was clearly a difficult situation for her. As he trailed after his big brother, he glanced back to find her chatting easily with Chelsea. Considering how the afternoon had started, he was relieved to see it was going to end up just fine.

"Okay, folks!" Mom called from the doorway. "Come and get it."

Everyone made a beeline for the dining room, and Jason positioned himself so Amy wouldn't get trampled in the crush. The sideboard was stocked with the average Barrett family spread, but when she got a good look at it, she laughed. "You're kidding, right?"

Following her openmouthed stare, he shrugged. "We Barretts go big, or we don't bother. The bonus is there's lots of leftovers to go around."

"That's not a problem for you," she commented as

she took a plate from the stack. "Your grandmother obviously feeds you well."

"That she does."

They chatted lightly while they filled their plates with everything from mac and cheese to a tender roast, but he couldn't miss the way she kept glancing over at Granddad. His frail condition prevented him from moving around on his own, and even though he had a perfectly good wheelchair, he despised using it. So they all took their seats around the huge dining table, with his hospital bed in its place at the head.

Gram made sure he had what he wanted, then pulled her chair up beside him. Ever since Jason could remember, they'd been that way, together through everything life had thrown at them. Even now, with his days slipping away, their touching devotion to each other was plain to see.

While his father said grace, a wave of sadness swept over Jason. This was a bittersweet Christmas for the Barretts, doubly so for him. If things had worked out the way he'd planned, he'd be sitting here with his wife. But the past was done and gone, and it was time to let it go. Making a vow to do just that, he added a heartfelt "Amen" at the end of Dad's prayer.

"Everything tastes even better than it smells," Amy announced with a smile for the cooks and another for their hosts. "Thank you so much for making me feel at home."

Gram returned the smile with a warm one of her own. "Jason's friends are always welcome here."

"Especially the single ones, right?" Amy teased.

"I have no idea what you're referring to, dear."

Grinning, Amy sipped her sweet tea but didn't say

anything more. Jason hadn't seen this part of her yet, and he had to admit it intrigued him. Up till now, she'd come across as an intense, creative type obsessed with perfection in everything she did. Discovering she had a playful side was like getting an early Christmas present.

Once they'd plowed through their meal, the family split into groups for various decorating assignments. With Christmas music playing from four sets of speakers located around the main floor, the work went by quickly. Outside, inside, everything was done up the way it had been for more years than Jason had been alive.

On the porches, pine garlands twined with lights swagged from the railings, and each window held a wreath tied with a burgundy velvet ribbon. Poinsettias sat on the tables, while red-and-green-plaid cushions had replaced the everyday ones on the wicker chairs and porch swing. Around it all, the three rooflines were rimmed in white lights that made the house look as if it was glowing with Christmas spirit.

When they were done, everyone took a few minutes to admire their handiwork and exchange high fives for getting it done without anyone falling off the roof. Then they all congregated around the tree Paul had trucked in from the woods surrounding the mill. Lots of people had fake ones these days, but to Jason, nothing said Christmas like the scents of a fresh-cut pine and gingerbread.

Jason and Amy stood near the fireplace, and she glanced at the collection of framed photos displayed there. A picture of the five teenage Barrett boys on a camping trip caught her eye, and she tapped one of the faces. "I haven't met him yet. Where does he live?"

His jaw tightened, but Jason reminded himself she couldn't possibly know she'd hit a nerve and did his best to sound casual. "That's my older brother, Scott. He's been in Texas the last five years."

She gave him an odd look but didn't press him for details. That was a good thing, because Scott was a very sore subject for all of them, and Jason didn't want anything to spoil this evening for his family.

Before they got started, Dad and Paul muscled Granddad's bed through the wide archway, parking it in front of the fireplace so he could supervise. The tree had always been his responsibility, and this year was no exception. Dad might have been the one on the ladder, but Granddad was in charge of telling him where the long strings of lights needed to be adjusted.

When they finally met his approval, Dad handed him the remote. "You do the honors, Pop."

"You checked all those bulbs?" he demanded.

"Every last one," Dad assured him with a chuckle. "Just like you taught me."

"All right, then."

He flipped the switch, and the massive tree shone with every color in the spectrum. It had gotten darker outside, so the lights were reflected in the angled glass of the bay window, enhancing the effect.

"Oh, kids," Gram breathed, "it's beautiful just like this."

They stood and admired it for about two seconds before his nieces and nephews dived into the ornament bins, snatching up their favorites and clamoring for Chelsea to put a hook on each one.

"I'd better go help her," Amy said, edging toward a small chair.

"Not trying to get away from me, are you?" Jason teased.

"Not a bit. In fact, I was hoping you might walk me home later."

"Hoping?" he echoed in mock disgust. Thickening his usual Virginia accent, he went on. "I'm a Southern gentleman, Miss Morgan. I've got no intention of letting you go off alone in the dark."

Picking up on his tone, she batted her eyes up at him. "I have always depended on the kindness of strangers."

"Blanche DuBois, *Streetcar Named Desire*." Judging by her delighted reaction, she hadn't expected him to know the reference. Grinning, he added, "Except I'm not a stranger."

Suddenly, her demeanor shifted, and her eyes darkened somberly. "But you're very kind, even to a demanding woman who drives most people crazy. That means more to me than you can possibly know."

Standing on tiptoe, she kissed his cheek and left him with a dazzling smile that drove deep into his heart, leaving behind a warm trail he suspected wouldn't be fading anytime soon.

Chapter Seven

By the time they were finished decorating the Barrett homestead, Amy knew each family member by name and was actually starting to feel like one of them. It wasn't hard to envision these generous, caring people giving an adopted child not only a home but a boisterous extended family. To her surprise, no one asked a single awkward question about what might be going on between Jason and her. She wasn't sure if that was because they were too polite to pry or if they already knew everything from the gossip flying around town.

Probably the second, she mused with a smile while she and Jason said their goodbyes. Aunt Helen stood proudly at the center of the local news chain, and while she'd never embarrass Amy, the chatty woman wasn't one to hold back anything juicy, either. And in a small, close-knit town like this, nothing was juicier than the prospect of a blossoming Christmas romance.

"Headed out?" Paul asked, holding up Chelsea's sweater for her to slip into.

"Yeah." Jason's grumbling was totally spoiled by

his troublemaker grin. "The boss wants me in extra early tomorrow."

Paul held up his hands in defense. "Hey, don't hassle me. If you weren't so good on the lathe, you'd get more time off."

Their good-natured argument continued while the four of them made the short walk through town to Arabesque. On the way, Jason asked Chelsea, "How're things going at your new place?"

"You mean, our old place," Chelsea corrected him, then explained to Amy, "We bought the old Garrison house on Ingram Street."

Amy searched her memory for the location. "You mean the one on the other side of the square?"

"That's the one," the newest Mrs. Barrett confirmed with a sigh. "It's a mess, but the price was right."

"Now we know why," Paul added grimly. "I thought the home inspector was kidding when he said the only good things were the foundation and the roof."

"Underneath all the ugly, it's still a lovely house," Chelsea assured them. "We just have to get it there."

Busy as they were at the mill, Amy admired their willingness to put so much effort into reclaiming the stately old Colonial. She was about to tell them that when she noticed Paul had stopped in the middle of the sidewalk and was staring at a pickup parked outside the Whistlestop. Because all the streetlights were on for holiday shoppers, it was easy to make out that it was dark green, with Idaho license plates. On the back bumper was a faded sticker that read "Ladies love country boys."

"Hey, Jason," he commented in a curious tone. "Isn't that your truck?"

Looking over, Jason scowled. "Sure is. They must've changed out the Oregon plates so the cops couldn't find it."

"So either Billy's here—"

"—or Rachel," Jason finished for him as the driver's door swung open and a petite—and very pregnant—woman stepped out.

Flipping long auburn hair over her shoulders, she arched her back in obvious discomfort and scanned the tiny business district with a helpless look. When her eyes landed on their group, they lit up with what Amy could only describe as joy.

For someone as front-heavy as she was, she moved pretty fast, and before anyone could react, she'd thrown herself at a flabbergasted Jason.

"Oh, Jason!" she choked out in a half sob. "I'm so glad to see you."

Moving like a man in a trance, he peeled her arms from around his neck and gently pushed her back. "How'd you find me?"

"I stopped in one of those internet cafés out on the highway and looked you up online. There's a bio of you on the Barrett's Mill Furniture website, and it was updated a couple weeks ago, so I was hoping you'd still be here."

The wonders of modern communication, Amy groused, wondering how Jason was going to handle this bizarre—and delicate—situation.

Giving his ex a disapproving once-over, he asked, "How's Billy?"

"Gone, months ago," she replied, her face twisting in anguish. "As soon as he found out about the baby, he was done with me. Hey, Paul," she added, as if she'd only just realized they weren't alone.

She didn't even glance at Chelsea or Amy, and Chelsea raised a disapproving brow. Paul settled an arm around her shoulders in an obvious attempt at keeping the peace. "Rachel McCarron, this is my wife, Chelsea."

She giggled at that, then seemed to register his somber expression. "Oh, you're serious. Sorry about that," she told Chelsea. "Back when I knew him, Paul wasn't exactly the marrying type."

Her thoughtless comment hung in the night air, which was growing chillier by the second.

Finally, Chelsea broke the tension. "We're on our way home, so we'll see you two later." She hugged both Jason and Amy, pointedly leaving out their unwelcome visitor. Wrapping Paul's arm around her shoulders, she angled him away and headed cross-lots to their house.

Sighing dramatically, Rachel watched them go. "She doesn't like me."

Chelsea adored Jason, and knowing what this woman had done to him couldn't sit well with her. Amy would be amazed if Chelsea's opinion of Rachel McCarron ever came close to thawing.

In truth, she hadn't been all that crazy about Jason's former fiancée even when Rachel was a distant memory for him. It had never occurred to Amy that they might actually meet someday. Or that she'd be pregnant and evidently in need of help. Then it hit her: Jason hadn't introduced them. After asking about Billy, he'd gone completely silent, as if he couldn't come up with anything more to say. Sadly, Rachel didn't share his affliction, but chattered along about this old friend and that one in a desperate attempt to fill the awkward silence.

When she finally stopped for breath, Amy seized what might be her only opportunity to air what she was thinking. Tapping his shoulder, she gave him a cool look. "Could I talk to you a minute?"

"Sure. Excuse me, Rachel."

Now he remembered his manners, Amy seethed while they moved a few yards away. She didn't know why she was so upset about his unexpected reunion with his ex, but her temper was simmering just beneath the surface, threatening to flare into an blistering tirade. Determined to avoid embarrassing them both, she took a deep breath to regain her composure.

Gazing down at her, he frowned. "What's wrong?"

"What's wrong?" she echoed furiously. "Are you serious?"

Patient as he usually was, she was stunned by the flash of anger in his eyes. "Look, this is a shock to me, too. You'll have to cut me some slack."

Most of the time, she gave in when people spoke to her that way. Then later, when she had a chance to think it over, she regretted allowing them to wipe their feet on her like some kind of doormat. Not this time, she vowed, pulling herself up to her full height and glaring at him for all she was worth. "By all means, take as much slack as you need. Good night."

Pivoting on her heel, she started across the street to where the cheery windows of Arabesque beckoned her inside where things still made sense to her. It was a fantasy, of course, but it was hers, and it was calling to her like the beacon marking a safe harbor.

Before she could reach it, Jason caught up with her and gently grasped her arm. When she yanked it free, he put up his hands in deference to her temper. "I shouldn't have done that, and I'm sorry. Please don't go off this way."

"What way?" she spat defiantly.

"Mad."

Stepping into an empty parking space, she folded her arms and scowled up at him. "Mad doesn't begin to cut it, mister."

"I'm confused. It's not my fault Rachel's here, y'know. I didn't ask her to come."

Clueless, she ranted silently, shaking her head. "Then I'll explain it to you. Paul introduced Chelsea to Rachel, but you left me standing there like the invisible woman."

By the startled look on his face, her complaint was news to him, and he hung his head like a woebegone hound. "I'm sorry. She caught me off guard, and my brain just shut off."

He looked so ashamed, she didn't have the heart to go on being angry at him. She understood his reaction, because she'd felt the same when she'd run into Devon shopping in Manhattan with his new girlfriend. *Uncomfortable* didn't even begin to describe the scene, and she recalled her tangled emotions vividly enough that she opted to give Jason a break.

"I guess I understand," she said, ducking to look at him. "And I apologize for overreacting."

His features brightened immediately.

"It's over between us, I promise. And that baby's not mine."

She'd figured that out for herself from their exchange about the absent Billy, but she appreciated him having the courage to meet the sensitive issue head-on. "What are you going to do?"

"I'm not sure," he confided with a glance over to

where Rachel stood waiting for him. "I'm guessing she needs somewhere to go, or she wouldn't have come all this way."

"What about her family?"

He grimaced. "She's from Iowa, and her parents are the conservative, buttoned-up type. They're probably not real thrilled with her right now."

Despite her initial reaction to Rachel's surprise visit, Amy couldn't help feeling sorry for her. Alone and pregnant, she'd driven across the country to the one person she thought she could count on. That it was Jason didn't surprise Amy in the least. That was the kind of guy he was, after all, and she'd certainly benefited from it herself.

Taking her hand, he fixed her with a pleading gaze. "It's a lot to take in, but I hope you can get your head around this. My no-good father left my mother to deal with her pregnancy and a baby when she was sixteen years old. If it hadn't been for the Barretts, who knows what would've happened to me? If Rachel needs my help, I'm gonna give it to her. It's the right thing to do."

While she still didn't like the situation one bit, Amy sensed he was appealing to her as a friend. Determined not to let Rachel get to her, she tamped down her irrational objections and did her best to appear calm. "I'm going home now. I'll be in my office doing the books, if you want to talk later."

He flashed her a little-boy grin. "Thanks."

With a quick "You're welcome," Amy gladly finished her walk to Arabesque. Fighting the urge to glance back at them, she unlocked the door to her apartment just as the vintage rotary phone on the counter began ringing. "Hello?"

"Who's that pregnant girl out there with Jason?" Aunt Helen demanded breathlessly.

"Are you using Uncle Fred's high-powered binoculars again?" she chided. "You know they're meant for bird-watching and spotting deer, right?"

"He's sound asleep, so he won't be missing them. Are you going to answer my question or not?"

Knowing she'd get the information one way or another, Amy decided to be helpful. "Rachel McCarron, his ex-fiancée from Oregon. And before you ask, the baby's not his."

She gave a very unladylike snort. "Of course it's not. He'd never leave the mother of his child to fend for herself like that."

While her aunt launched into a melodramatic assessment of other local couples in dicey situations, Amy was astonished to discover she didn't doubt his claim for even a single moment. As a performer, she'd learned to be wary of people's intentions, never taking anyone at face value because most of the characters around her were superb actors. Because of that, she had a hard time believing anyone until she'd known them for a long time.

Somehow, Jason had earned her trust very quickly, and she took it on faith that he was being straight with her.

An interesting change, she thought while she *mmm-hmm*ed and *uh-huh*ed at the right spots in their one-way conversation. She didn't know the dictionary definition of *faith,* but she understood it basically meant believing in something you couldn't see or touch.

She believed Jason, but did she also believe *in* him? She hadn't considered that before, but she had to admit she probably did. She certainly felt he'd been honest with her, right from their first meeting through tonight. He was funny and sweet, and he had a way of making her feel special without saying a word.

"Don't you think so?" Aunt Helen asked, finally dragging Amy back into the discussion.

"Absolutely." Since she hadn't heard the question, she hoped her response made sense.

"A good boy, through and through. And from what Olivia tells me, he really likes you. You could do worse."

I have, Amy thought grimly. But over the past few days, Jason had convinced her she deserved better, and at some point she'd started to agree with him. "Aunt Helen, I hate to cut you off, but I really should get going on the books."

"Oh, listen to me, rattling along when you've got work to do. You go on, and I'll see you soon."

Adding a noisy air kiss, she hung up. Amy disconnected with a relieved sigh. She adored the woman, but an extended chat with her could be exhausting. Normally, she detested opening her bookkeeping program and logging everything in, but after the hectic day she'd had, she was actually looking forward to sitting down at her desk for some Mozart and number crunching.

After watching Amy to make sure she'd gotten inside all right, Jason cast a hesitant look over at Rachel. For the life of him, he didn't know what to say. Jamming his hands into the pockets of his jeans, he trudged back to where she was waiting, searching his uncooperative brain for a way to start a conversation he'd never anticipated having. When she took off nearly a year ago, it had taken him a while to accept she was really gone. Once he did, though, he'd assumed he'd never see her again.

But here she was, and he had to come up with a way to deal with it. Inspiration struck, and he asked, "Are you hungry?"

"Starving," she replied in a voice tinged with desperation. "I put the last of my money in the gas tank this morning."

Jason had a hard time accepting that someone in her family wouldn't at least send her some cash. "Do your parents know about the baby?"

"Sure they do. They offered to help me 'take care of it.'" She spat the words with disdain. "When I refused, they told me never to call them again."

The bitterness in her voice wavered, and her dark eyes filled with tears. Jason wondered if his mother had faced the same heartlessness from her own family and gave him up to make sure he'd be raised by people who would always love him, no matter how badly he messed up.

His instinct was to gather Rachel into his arms and comfort her, but he didn't want to create the wrong impression for her or the curious eyes he assumed were watching this little drama unfold. Instead, he took her hands and gave them a reassuring squeeze.

"Rachel, look at me." When he had her attention, he steeled himself against her tears and tried to think practically. "First, we're gonna go inside and get you something to eat. Next, I'll find you a place to stay the night, and tomorrow we'll figure out what to do."

Sniffling, she blinked up at him in obvious confusion. "You mean, you're going to help me?"

"Did you come all this way thinking I wouldn't?"

"I was hoping." He opened the door of the Whistle-stop for her, and the scent of good Southern cooking spilled out into the night air. Taking a deep breath, she sighed. "That smells incredible."

The place was about half-full, and he led her to a booth near the back where they could talk in relative privacy. After the waitress took her order, Rachel reached across the table to take one of his hands. "Thank you, Jason. I know this must be really hard for you, after the way things ended with us."

Glancing down, he noticed the fingers on both her hands were bare. It hadn't been much of a diamond, but it had been the most expensive thing he'd ever bought that didn't have tires and a steering wheel. "Sold the ring, huh?"

Nodding, she frowned. "I'm sorry."

By the misery clouding her features, he believed she meant it. Once he'd taken that in, he realized that if she kept apologizing to him, they'd both have to relive their failed engagement over and over. He saw no point in doing that, so he forced a smile. "You can quit saying you're sorry. I forgave you a long time ago."

"You did?" When he nodded, she gave him a forlorn look. "How could you, when I haven't forgiven myself?"

The Rachel McCarron he'd known had never regretted anything. A free spirit in every sense of the word, she'd appealed to him for just that reason. Beautiful and untamed, she'd been driven by the wind to wherever she was headed next. At the time, the fact that she'd chosen to settle with him made him so proud, he'd ignored Paul's warnings about her, along with the ones in the back of his own mind.

At first, Jason had often pictured seeing her again,

imagining what they might say to each other. As the months went by, those images had faded, and now all he felt for her was sympathy.

Once she had her food, he smiled to ease the sorrow clouding her face. "That was a long time ago, and it's best to leave it in the past. Now, eat up."

Digging into her meat loaf, she hummed in appreciation. "This is awesome! It reminds me of that great little diner in Oregon you and Paul used to take me to. Who does the cooking here?"

"Molly Harkness. She and her husband, Bruce, have been keeping the town well fed since before I was born."

"Do you think they need any kitchen help?" Rachel asked after wolfing down another bite. "I could wash dishes or something."

Jason eyed her pregnant frame doubtfully. Slender as she usually was, he thought, all that extra weight must be murder for her to carry around. The last thing she needed was to be on her feet all day. "When're you due?"

"January twentieth." Swallowing some milk, she added a wry grin. "Great way to start the new year, right?"

"Could be." Chewing on that for a few seconds, he had a brainstorm. "Lemme check around town, explain your situation. Maybe someone's got some light work you could manage."

"Do you really think anyone here will hire me? I mean, this is your hometown. They must all know how badly I treated you."

More remorse, he thought. Maybe impending motherhood had forced her to mature a little and own up to her failings. Whatever the reason, it was definitely a step in the right direction. "These are good folks, and they've all made mistakes, too. I can't promise anything, but I'll try."

"That's more than I could ask for," she said with a grateful smile. "Thank you."

"The Donaldsons here on Main Street have an apartment out back in an old carriage house. Paul and Chelsea moved out when they bought their house, and it's still empty. It's small, but the rent's cheap, and it'd be all yours. Plus, Hank and Lila would be nearby if you needed something."

"When I said I have no money, I meant none at all," she protested meekly. "If I can't get a job, that's not going to change anytime soon."

"Let's just ask and see what they say." Pulling out his cell phone, he made the call and got the response he'd expected.

"Oh, that poor thing, and at Christmastime, too. Bring her over, Jason," Lila said without hesitation. "I'll send Hank out to raise the heat and turn on the lights. We'll work out the details later."

"Thanks, Lila. We'll be there in a few minutes."

While he paid the check, his gut was warning him to put some distance between himself and this particular damsel in distress. Amy's baffling reaction to Rachel's sudden appearance kept popping into his mind, and he resolved to smooth things over with her once he got Rachel settled. Women were complex, and it was best never to lose sight of that. If that meant a longer night than usual, Jason suspected in the long run it would be easier than trying to mend fences with one woman over helping another.

In the space of an evening, his life had gotten very

complicated. He only prayed he could deal with the molehills before they became mountains.

Jason helped Rachel into the cab of the truck he'd thought he'd never see again and climbed in beside her. The interior was a disaster, and on the rear jump seat sat a single duffel bag.

"Have you been living in here?" he asked. When she nodded, he bit back a curse. "If I ever get my hands on Billy…"

"Please don't," she whimpered, closing her eyes and leaning her head against the window. "I don't even want to think about that nasty piece of work. I just want to curl up in a ball on a real bed and go to sleep."

In response, he started the truck and saw the low-fuel light was on. Fortunately, they didn't have far to go, so he made the short drive up the street to the Donaldson place. Just as Lila had promised, the carriage house was bright and inviting when he grabbed Rachel's bag and carefully walked her down the pathway to the front door.

Standing in front of it, she stared at the simple cottage with large, tear-filled eyes. Then she lowered her head and folded her hands in prayer. When she was finished, she looked up at him with an awed expression. "It doesn't seem like enough, but thank you."

"You're welcome." Opening the door for her, he followed her inside. "Where do you want your stuff?"

"Anywhere," she answered, sinking onto the bed with a weary sigh.

Realizing she needed someone to take care of things for her, he left the bag on the floor of the single closet.

"So, the bathroom's through there—" he pointed

"—and this is the kitchen." When he opened the fridge, it was empty, and he frowned. "That's not good."

"The story of my life."

This defeated young woman was nothing like the vibrant, fearless Rachel he'd once known. Hopelessness did that to people, he knew, and he searched for a way to bring back even a sliver of her old optimism. Sliding his wallet from his back pocket, he thumbed through the cash he'd taken out of his account to buy Christmas presents. Removing half of it, he set it on the tiny kitchen table.

"I can't take your money," she objected instantly. "After what I did to you, I couldn't live with myself."

"It's not for you," he reasoned in a stern tone very unlike him. Because of his own sketchy history, there was no way he'd be backing down on this one. "It's for your baby. You've got a month to go, and if it's gonna be born healthy, you have to eat right and take care of yourself. That little one's counting on you, and you're in no position to choose your pride over food."

She gave him a wan smile. "You're right, but I'll pay you back. I promise."

She'd made promises to him before that hadn't worked out, so he tucked this one away with a nod. If she ended up repaying him, he'd be happy. If not, he'd take it in stride. That was how things worked with Rachel; he'd learned that the hard way. She wasn't a bad person, but she wasn't all that reliable when it came to following through. He prayed motherhood would change that, but only time would tell.

"The bathroom's stocked, and the bed's made," he said as he edged toward the door. "Need anything else?"

"Just a solid night's sleep." Peeling back the covers, she slid beneath them and closed her eyes.

"Then I'll say good-night. I've gotta work in the morning, but I'll make some calls during my breaks and see if anyone's looking for help during the holidays. Sound good?"

"Mmm-hmm."

Since she was clearly too exhausted to take care of the lights, he flipped the switches, leaving the night-light in the bathroom on for her. There was a set of keys on the table, which he left for her. Setting the lock, he pulled the door shut behind him and headed back up the walkway. Inside the house, he noticed Lila standing in the kitchen window and held up his hand in thanks. She acknowledged him with a nod and turned off the light.

Keeping an eye on him, he mused with a grin. While he hadn't doubted their reaction to Rachel's plight, he appreciated Hank and Lila proving his claim that the residents of Barrett's Mill were good, helpful folks. As a single, expectant mother, Rachel needed all the grace she could get.

After a quick debate, he decided to leave his filthy truck where it was until he could give it a thorough cleaning inside and out. When he got to Arabesque, he noticed the lights were still on and knocked at the front door.

Stepping aside to let him in, Amy asked, "How did it go?"

"Which part?" He grinned, hoping to ease some of the tension he heard in her voice.

"Whichever part you want to tell me about," she hedged, leading him back to her cozy office.

Decorated in classical theater and ballet posters, it

reminded him of old movies where a character's luggage was plastered with stickers from other countries. As foreign to him as those faraway places, the designs were Amy's style, wrapping up her eventful life like colorful paper on a gift.

"I just heated water for tea," she said as he settled into one of the threadbare velvet chairs. "Would you like some decaf coffee?"

"That'd be great." In less than a minute, he had a steaming mug in his hands and took a long, appreciative sip. "Delicious."

"I'm glad you like it."

They traded a few more overly polite comments, and he stifled a groan. He'd gotten accustomed to the warm back-and-forth he enjoyed with Amy, and this was as far from it as he could get. It hadn't occurred to him that his encounter with Rachel would affect Amy so much, and he resolved to set things to rights as quickly as humanly possible.

"So," he began, setting down his half-empty cup. "Should I start with Rachel past or Rachel present?"

Amy shrugged, but those gorgeous blue eyes darkened ominously. He didn't know what the color shift meant, but he instinctively didn't like it. So he spilled the whole crazy story, from the day he first met Rachel singing at a Renaissance fair in Seattle, to their months living in Oregon, to her pulling into Barrett's Mill in his stolen truck. When he was finished, he forced himself to smile. "So, that's everything."

Without saying anything, she drank some of her tea and deliberately put her dainty china cup on its saucer next to the hefty mug she'd offered him. Pinning him with a direct stare, she asked, "How do you feel about seeing her again?"

He suspected she was fishing for something, but he had no idea what she was after. "I'm not sure what you mean."

"She took off with a man you considered a friend, stole your truck and the ring you gave her." To emphasize, she ticked Rachel's sins off on her slender fingers. "Now she's come crawling into town, asking you to help her? She's either completely destitute or she's got an awful lot of nerve."

"Actually, it's both."

"Oh, Jason," she lamented with a pained expression. "Tell me you didn't give her any money."

"She's got nothing but a duffel bag and a baby who needs to be fed somehow. What was I supposed to do?"

"You left the truck at the Donaldsons', didn't you?" When he nodded, she sighed. "What's to keep her from taking off again?"

Feeling quite proud of himself, he reached into his pocket and dangled the keys for her to see. "Unless she's learned how to hot-wire an ignition, she's not going anywhere."

Amy's frown gave way to a smile, and she clapped quietly. "Very well played."

"Thank you, thank you. I'll be here all month." They both laughed, and he was relieved to have gotten through the tough part. "So are we okay?"

Tilting her head, she studied him through narrowed eyes. He knew her wariness was driven by Devon's betrayal and not anything Jason had done, but it still bugged him. Someday, he hoped he'd see nothing but joy in those stunning blue eyes of hers. "I'll be honest—

I'm not crazy about this whole scenario. But I admire you for stepping up to give a hand to someone who seems to have no one else to turn to."

She didn't trust Rachel, he realized. For some reason, the fact that Amy was so protective of him made him feel incredible. People assumed a big, strong guy like him could take care of himself, and aside from his family, no one worried about him all that much. Tiny as she was, he'd gained a sincere respect for how formidable an opponent Amy could be when she put her mind to it.

"There's nothing to admire in this," he corrected her. "It's the right thing to do."

"Just don't let her take advantage of you like she did before," Amy warned him with a stern look. "I might have to hurt her."

Her threat made him chuckle. "I'll keep that in mind."

"I'm serious, you big oaf. Women like Rachel sail through life wrapping men around their little fingers and gouging them for everything they've got. Then, when the mood strikes, poof!" She illustrated her point with an intricate waving of fingers that was easy to interpret.

"I'll keep that in mind, too," Jason assured her as they both stood. "It sure is comforting to know you've got my back."

"Someone needs to watch out for you." She gave him an indulgent smile. "You're too nice for your own good."

"Guess I wouldn't last long in the big city, huh?"

"Half an hour, tops."

Gazing down at her, he took in the intelligence sparkling in her eyes, the set of her delicate jaw. She might look as if she was made of porcelain, but under all that polish ran a streak of steely determination that appealed to him just as much. "Then it's a good thing you ended up here. Otherwise we never would've met."

Smiling, he reached out to smooth a stray lock of hair back into her loose ponytail. The motion took his fingers across her soft skin, and he cradled her cheek in his hand. Because he couldn't help himself, he leaned in and brushed a kiss over her lips. That brief connection to her did something strange to his heart, which suddenly felt as if it meant to pound its way out of his chest.

Startled by the intensity of his reaction to her, he pulled back and watched her eyes blink open with the same bewildered look he must be wearing. Assuming he'd pushed too far too fast, he stammered, "Amy, I'm s—"

She cut off his apology by pulling him in for another, much longer kiss. For a few moments, he rode that wave of emotions, gathering her in, savoring the way her slender frame fit against him. Then, because he was a gentleman, he drew away and held her at arm's length.

Figuring humor would give him the best exit, he said, "Thanks for the coffee."

That got him the laugh he'd been hoping for, and she waved him off. "You're welcome. And if anyone asks, it was the mistletoe."

She pointed at the kissing ball dangling from the ceiling, but he still didn't know what she was referring to. Then he noticed the bare window that looked into her office. It didn't take a genius to know some busybody had seen that kiss and was quickly spreading the word. "Gotcha. 'Night, Amy."

He was on his way out the door when she said, "Sweet dreams, Sir Galahad."

Flattening his palm on the doorjamb, he poked his head back in. "What? I'm not Lancelot?"

"His affair with Guinevere destroyed Arthur and then Camelot," she explained. "Galahad was known for pure gallantry, expecting nothing in return. That's you."

He'd gotten his share of compliments from women over the years, but none had the impact of this one. "I had no idea you saw me that way."

"I know." Shaking her head, she gave him an approving smile. "That's what makes you so special."

Amy thought he was special, Jason mused as he let himself out the studio door. Replaying the kiss that had nearly knocked him over, he couldn't help grinning as he strolled toward his grandparents' house. He'd never really considered himself anything out of the ordinary, but Amy had seen a lot more of the world than he had. Not to mention, she'd come into contact with more people, not all of them nice. That was where her cynicism came from, he realized. The fact that a small-town boy like him had captured her interest was incredibly flattering.

Then again, Devon had been one of those worldly guys she'd known, and he'd let her down in the worst way imaginable. Abandoning someone who needed you was something Jason simply couldn't understand. As he arrived home, he made a silent vow.

Whatever happened between Amy and him, he'd always put her wishes before his own. No matter how much it might hurt.

Chapter Eight

"Tell me everything," Brenda insisted before Amy had even sat down for their pre-Christmas shopping breakfast. "Don't leave anything out."

"There's really not much to tell," Amy hedged, opening the menu hoping to appear nonchalant. "Rachel Mc-Carron drove into town last night on fumes."

"And bursting at the seams," Brenda supplied helpfully.

As she stacked her hands and rested her chin on them, Amy's eyes were drawn to the rings on her left hand. They weren't flashy, but the gold and modest diamond setting caught the overhead lights in a pretty display. Amy had only gotten half a set herself, and she'd felt compelled to return the diamond when her engagement ended. Rachel hadn't, though, she groused silently. According to Jason, she'd sold it at a pawnshop somewhere in Colorado.

"Hello? Earth to Amy."

"Sorry. What were you saying?"

As if on cue, Molly Harkness stopped at their table. The best cook within a hundred miles, she had five kids, fourteen grandkids and the sharpest ears in town. "She was saying she doesn't know what you're thinking, leaving Jason alone with his ex that way."

"What was I supposed to do?" Amy demanded in exasperation. "It's not like we're a couple or anything. And even if we were, I'd never step in where I'm not wanted."

"I would," Brenda declared without hesitation. "I'd protect what's mine before Bambi got any bright ideas. Rare as that might be," she added with a giggle.

"Honey, she's right." Molly patted her shoulder in a gesture that was obviously meant to be supportive but just ended up making Amy feel as if they were ganging up on her.

"Rachel's pregnant," she reminded them both more curtly than she'd intended. "If I make a fuss over her, he'll think I'm awful."

The other two women traded a grim look, and Molly sighed. "You've hit the nail on that one. A good breakfast oughta help the thinking along. What would you girls like?"

Brenda ordered her usual platter with everything but the kitchen sink, but the idea of food made Amy's stomach roll over in protest. "I'll just have the fruit plate."

"Farmer's breakfast it is," Molly vetoed her, hustling off while Amy was still sputtering her objections.

"Just go with it, Ames," Brenda advised while she sugared her coffee and handed the dispenser across the table. "Molly's seen everything at least once, and she's always right."

"I guess." Feeling dejected, Amy stirred her coffee, watching the creamer and sugar swirl around in the cup. The music playing on the diner's speakers changed tracks, and the opening of "I'll Be Home for Christmas" made her smile. "I love this song. This year, it really fits me, doesn't it?"

"I'm so glad you're back home again," Brenda gushed, reaching over to pat her hand. "You always were my favorite cousin. I remember when Mom and I used to drive to Washington to see you dance in those productions. I'd sit in the audience and hold my breath the whole time you were onstage, praying you wouldn't mess up."

"I did a few times," Amy confided.

"I never noticed. To me, you were flawless."

"Not so much anymore." The words slipped out before she could stop them, and she fiddled with her napkin to avoid meeting her cousin's gaze.

"It's okay, you know," Brenda said gently. "Being imperfect is what makes us human. It helps us sympathize with other people's weaknesses."

"Such as?"

"Such as Jason Barrett's heart is bigger than it needs to be. Which is probably why he's bringing that car thief in here for breakfast." When Amy angled to look, Brenda ordered, "Don't you dare. If he wants to see you, he'll come over on his own. Don't for one second let her think she bothers you. He's interested in you now, not her."

"Do you really think so?" Amy asked.

"Did he kiss you last night or not?"

Amy narrowed her eyes in annoyance. "I didn't tell you that."

"Don't be dense," she scolded with a laugh. "If you don't want folks knowing your business, put a curtain on that window in your office."

A server dropped off their plates, giving Amy time

to regain her perspective. Before diving into her eggs, she grinned. "It was the mistletoe."

"Good excuse," Brenda approved through a mouthful of home fries. "Seeing as it's Christmas and all."

"Speaking of which, what do your kids want to find under the tree on the big day?"

In response, Brenda reached into her purse and pulled out a sheaf of lined notebook paper, which she handed to Amy. At the top of each was one of her kids' names, followed by a long list of wishes.

Flipping through them, Amy laughed. "It's a good thing we get along so well. Looks like it's gonna be a long day."

Even from a distance, Amy Morgan was still the prettiest thing Jason had ever seen.

Fortunately for him, Rachel was too hungry to talk much, so he just let her eat while he tried to watch Amy without letting on that he was staring at her. She and Brenda were chatting and laughing, apparently oblivious to the other folks in the dining room. Considering the unpleasant tasks he had ahead of him this morning, he'd much rather have been starting his day out with their lively company.

But he wasn't, so he'd just have to make the best of it. His restless night had left him tired and cranky, which wasn't helpful when what he needed was to be patient and understanding.

Summoning his usual optimism, he started what could only be an awkward conversation. "So, when's the last time you saw a doctor?"

Chewing on some toast, she considered that for long enough to make him very nervous. "San Antonio."

He bit back a sarcastic comment and tried again. "When was that?"

"A couple weeks ago. It was a clinic, and the nurse said everything looked fine to her."

"I'd feel better if Doc Peterson checked you over. Y'know, make sure everything's okay."

"Doctors are expensive," she reminded him, as if he'd forgotten.

"He and my dad go way back, so I'm sure he'll do us a favor."

"Okay."

She shrugged as if it didn't matter to her, and alarm bells went off in Jason's head. "Are you all right?"

"It's just…"

Her voice trailed off into some minor waterworks, and she dropped her face in her hands. Worst-case scenario, he groaned inwardly as people at the tables nearby politely turned their heads away from the heart-wrenching scene near the window. Completely out of his depth, Jason searched for a way to comfort her. Or at the very least make her quit crying.

Then, as suddenly as they'd appeared, the tears stopped. With a shaky breath, she gave him a wan smile. "Sorry about that. Sometimes it catches up with me, how alone we are."

She rested a protective hand over her stomach, and he marveled at how much she'd changed since he'd known her in Oregon. While he hated to consider what she'd gone through before reaching Barrett's Mill, he was glad to know her restlessness was a thing of the past. "Once you feel settled, things'll get better."

"You think?"

"I know."

"You were always so sweet."

When tears started welling up again, he stopped her with a hand in the air. "If you're fixing to apologize again, save your breath."

"Okay." Her eyes drifted over to the booth where Amy and Brenda had their heads together over a pile of notebook paper. "She's really pretty."

"Yeah, she is. She's also a great teacher, and her students love her."

Rachel's gaze swung back to him with sudden interest. "What about you? Do you love her, too?"

Did he? He hadn't known Amy that long, and they were so different. But he couldn't deny that they'd clicked that first day, and he had a very hard time getting her out of his thoughts long enough to concentrate on anything else. He loved the graceful way she moved, the light, flowery scent of her perfume, even the way she went toe-to-toe with him over necessary mechanical changes to her set design.

She definitely intrigued him, and it wouldn't take much for him to fall hard for her. But love? As he considered the woman sitting across from him, he realized he hadn't moved as far on as he'd assumed. Rachel had broken more than his heart. She'd shattered his trust in himself, in his ability to let go and simply let himself feel.

Because he wasn't willing to explore that any further on a couple of hours' sleep, he dug into his cooling omelet and changed the subject. "So, you said your last job was singing at a bar in Phoenix. I'm thinking that's not such a good option for you now."

That got him a rueful grin, which was a big step up. "Ladies and gentlemen, Jason Barrett, the master of understatement."

He laughed, but abruptly stopped when he noticed Amy and Brenda headed their way. Any guy with a brain could guess how this was going to go, and he wasn't looking forward to the collision.

Standing, he dredged up his best smile. "'Morning, ladies."

"Jason." Brenda sniffed, giving Rachel a suspicious look before offering her hand. "I'm Brenda Lattimore. Welcome to Barrett's Mill."

Her chilly greeting had the ring of a cobra inviting a mouse into range, and Amy rolled her eyes with a sigh. "How are you doing this morning, Rachel? I hope you slept well."

"It's much better than sleeping in the truck."

Brenda's flinty look dissolved, and her mother's instincts took over. "Oh, you poor thing! How awful."

"I'm just grateful to be here with nice people around who care about what happens to me and my baby."

"So are we," Amy assured her with a warmth that couldn't be faked. "Every child should come into the world knowing they're loved."

Jason sensed she was including him in that gracious comment, and he silently thanked her for it. Overcome by gratitude for her understanding, it was all he could do not to kiss her right there in front of everyone. "What are you ladies up to today?"

"Christmas shopping." Those soft lips curved flirtatiously, and she added, "Would you like me to add in anything for you?"

Returning that smile was the most natural thing he'd ever done. "Nope. I got everything I want."

"All right, you two," Brenda jumped in, pulling her cousin away. "Save it for under the mistletoe. Bye, now."

Still standing, Jason watched them stroll down the sidewalk toward the shops so lavishly decorated for the holidays. He kept them in sight until they turned a corner, then stifled a sigh as he sat back down.

"I don't care what you say," Rachel told him with the authority of an expert. "You're in love with her. The good news is, she feels the same way about you."

"You're nuts. We just met."

"Oh, that doesn't matter even the teeniest little bit," she informed him while she salted her eggs. "When two people go together, that's it. Logic has nothing to do with it."

"I thought *we* went together."

"No, you didn't," she corrected him quietly. "You tried to make it happen, because more than anything you want a family of your own to love and take care of. Your mistake was trying to fit me into that box."

"And what makes you think Amy's open to being in the box with me?"

"I'm a woman," she reminded him with a coy smile. "We always know."

Jason chewed on that for a minute, then decided she might be right. But even if Amy already knew how she felt about him, he wouldn't be surprised if it took her a while to own up to it. They'd both gotten burned in the past, and that would make it tougher for them to take that step again.

But anything was possible. After all, it was Christmastime.

Amy was getting ready for choir practice when someone started honking out front. Grabbing a light jacket, she went through the studio and saw a minivan waiting outside the large bay window.

Brenda.

I should have known, she thought as she let herself out the front door and locked it behind her.

Pausing on the sidewalk, she glanced back to admire the festive look she and Jason had created to draw people into Arabesque. Even if she'd worked at it for months, she couldn't have designed a better representation of both the studio and the show. Odd as it seemed, they made a great team, her with the ideas and him with the practical experience to bring them to life.

When she climbed in beside her cousin, she chided, "You really didn't have to do this. I would've met you there."

"It's no big deal. You're on my way."

Right. Any other day, she might have continued the debate just for fun, but thinking about Jason had left her feeling generous, so she let it drop. "I wrapped the kids' gifts last night. Do you want to stop and get them after rehearsal so you can put them under your tree?"

"Not a chance," Brenda replied as she parked in the church's lot. "They'll shake and nudge and peek until they end up opening them 'by mistake.'" She punctuated this with air quotes and laughed. "It's safer to hang on to them and bring them Christmas morning."

"Will do." They got out of the van, and Amy said, "I can't believe how many people are here. The lot's almost as full as it was on Sunday."

"The difference is, most of us are here alone," Brenda pointed out as they went up the steps. "On Sunday, those same cars are full of people."

"Is that why you do this? To get some time to yourself?"

"Pretty much. I love my kids to pieces, but I have to get some me time once in a while or I'll go bonkers."

In her wistful tone, Amy heard a desperate plea for a break. She'd been trying to come up with a gift for her vivacious cousin, and the lightbulb went off: spa day. There had to be one around here somewhere, she reasoned. It occurred to her that Chelsea Barrett would be the kind of woman who'd know something like that, and she made a mental note to call and ask her.

The buzz of voices inside the chapel dragged her back to the present, and she braced herself to go through the open double doors. Sunday had gone well, but for some reason she was nervous about tonight. She'd never suffered from stage fright when she was dancing, but singing in front of so many people was a different thing altogether.

"You'll be fine," Brenda whispered encouragingly, giving her a quick squeeze around the shoulders. "It's Christmas music, so just hit as many notes as you can. That's what most of us will be doing, anyway."

Amy laughed, and behind her a familiar voice drawled, "I like the way this is goin' already."

She spun to find Jason standing there, wearing a grin that made her glad there was no mistletoe around. If there was, even though they were in church she might not have been able to resist stealing a kiss. "How are you tonight?"

The grin deepened, and for the first time she noticed a dimple in his tanned cheek. "Better now."

"I think someone's looking for me," Brenda announced, winking at Amy before flouncing away.

"She never was subtle, your cousin."

"Cheerleaders usually aren't," Amy pointed out. She debated asking about Rachel, then decided if she didn't, he'd think she was avoiding the subject. Beyond that, remaining in the dark would make her crazy. "How's Rachel doing?"

"As well as you could expect. Turns out Doc Peterson's receptionist quit, and he needed someone to fill in through the holidays till he can hire someone permanently. It's easy, sitting-down work, which is good. Rachel's not all that organized, but she's decent with the computer and on the phone, so it's a good solution for now."

And then what? Amy was dying to ask, but Mrs. Griggs was calling everyone into the sanctuary, so her answer would have to wait.

Amy eyed the risers hesitantly. There were no handrails, and because of her limited mobility, the vertical distance was a little high for her. She didn't want to make a fool of herself by falling in front of everyone.

In his usual way, Jason came to her rescue, offering his arm. When she was safely standing in the soprano section, she thanked him.

"Anytime."

Once he'd moved on, Brenda popped up next to her and said, "I forgot my music. Can I share with you?"

"Sure." Amy opened her folder of music and held it so they could both see.

As the pianist began playing the opening chords of "Hark the Herald Angels Sing," Brenda murmured, "Just for future reference, I make an excellent matron of honor."

Out of respect for the pastor's wife, Amy simply

shook her head. Despite the overly sentimental rumors flying around town, she and Jason were a long way from choosing a wedding party. In fact, after the disastrous way his last engagement had ended, she wouldn't be at all surprised to learn that he wasn't keen to get serious with anyone. That should have been a huge relief to her, since she wasn't interested in a relationship, either.

But for some strange reason it just made her sad.

Jason was totally focused on turning a spindle for the back of the rocking chair he was working on, so he didn't realize he had company until his ear protectors disappeared. "What the—"

The rest of his protest trailed off as Jenna Reed dragged him through the workshop and out the back door of the mill house. By his ear.

When she decided they were far enough from the rest of the crew, she let him go, giving him a firm shove for good measure. "What's wrong with you?"

"Well, my ear kinda hurts." Rubbing it, he glared back at her. "What's your problem?"

Today, her faded denim overalls were covered in stone dust, which told him something of major importance had interrupted her chiseling time. "Are you a complete idiot?"

"Sometimes." He added a grin, but she merely planted her hands on her hips while the glare hardened into an unforgiving scowl. Sensing humor wasn't the right approach, he spread his hands in a calming gesture. "I give. What's up?"

"What'd I tell you about Amy?"

"That she's been hurt enough, and I should be careful. Which I'm doing."

"Then how come a customer just told me you've been cozying up with Amy at her place?"

"You hate gossip," Jason reminded her. "Since when do you listen to anything like that?"

"Since it involves a very good friend—" she narrowed her eyes "—and you."

He laughed. "Gimme a break. You make me sound like the Big Bad Wolf going after Little Red Riding Hood."

"Are you?"

The insult stung, and he bit back some pretty harsh words. Something was going on here, and while he didn't understand it, he decided it was best not to further provoke her by retaliating. "You know me better than that."

"Do I? I've been here six months, and in all that time, I've never seen you with the same girl for more than a couple weeks."

She had him there, Jason had to admit, but Amy wasn't like those other women. The more time he spent with her, the more she fascinated him. Usually, a few dates were enough to convince him it was time to move on. Between the show and other holiday goings-on around town, he and Amy saw each other every day, and he eagerly looked forward to connecting with her. In fact, he wouldn't have minded if they spent even more time together.

He wasn't ready to share those feelings with anyone else, so he shrugged. "Amy's different."

"How?" Leaning against a nearby tree, Jenna folded her arms with a curious expression. It beat the looks she'd been giving him, and he relaxed a little.

"She's smart and funny," he began, then couldn't

keep back a smile. "And she's still the prettiest thing I've ever seen."

"Prettier than Rachel?"

"To me, she is."

"Spare me," Jenna scoffed. "Even eight months pregnant, Rachel's gorgeous. I can't imagine how she is on a normal day."

Being male, he couldn't deny she held the more obvious appeal. But Amy's appearance was more refined, and she had an elegant style no woman he'd ever met could match. More reserved by nature, she kept a lot to herself, and that only made her more captivating to him. While he considered how to explain his preference, something clicked into place for him, and he smiled. "Guess I outgrew Barbie dolls. Now I want something else."

"Meaning Amy?"

"Maybe," he allowed, still unwilling to discuss this with Jenna when he hadn't brought it up with the lady in question. "But only if that's what she wants. We're about as different as two people can get, and I've got no plans to change. I'm figuring she doesn't, either. Which is fine with me, 'cause I think she's perfect the way she is."

"I'm not big on compromise myself, so I get that." Apparently satisfied with the result of her interrogation, she pushed off from the tree. "Okay, I'm going. But you watch your step, JB. I've got my eye on you."

"Good to know," he tossed back, getting a smack on the shoulder in reply. While he watched her get into her van, his cell phone vibrated in his pocket. Pulling it out, he saw the caller ID and answered. "Hey, Mom. What's up?"

"I'm with your grandparents, and we need you here right now."

The line went dead before he could ask for details, and his pulse shot into the stratosphere. Going back inside to explain would only waste time, so he ran for his truck, dialing as he went. "Chelsea, I'm headed to Gram and Granddad's. Tell Paul."

He ground the engine into gear and flew down the pitted lane, ducking reflexively from the stones pelting his windows. It couldn't be Granddad, logic told him, or Mom would've called in Paul and Chelsea, too. That meant something had happened to Gram, and Jason pulled in long, deep breaths to combat the dread seizing his heart. He took one curve a little too fast and frantically steered the truck back onto the dirt road. Easing back on the gas, he reminded himself he couldn't help anyone if he crashed into a tree on the way into town.

The drive felt twice as long as on a normal day, but he finally made it home. Leaving his door open and the cranky engine running, he ran up the front steps and into the dining room. Granddad was even paler than usual, and he pointed toward the kitchen. "They're in there."

"Is Gram okay?"

"More or less. I tried to get up and help them, but they won't let me."

Jason realized his panic was the last thing anyone needed to see right now, so he forced calm into his voice. "Can I get you anything?"

"I'm fine. See to your grandmother."

He didn't look fine, but Jason obeyed him out of habit. In the kitchen, he found the two women who'd raised him sitting on the floor. Gram's arm was at an odd angle, resting on an overturned pot padded with towels.

Hunkering down, he summoned a little humor. "I've heard those things work better upright on the stove."

"Oh, you," Gram chided him in a shaky voice that scared him down to his boots. Resolute and strong, she inspired the Barrett family with her faith and unrelenting optimism. Seeing her this way was a stark warning that in a heartbeat, things he'd relied on his entire life could change.

Firmly shutting the negative thought away, he glanced around and noticed a three-step stool on its side. Obviously, she'd wanted something from one of the high cupboards and needed the stool to reach it. Even though he knew it was pointless, he felt awful for not being there. "You couldn't wait for me?"

"Don't you be giving me those guilty eyes, young man. You were at work, and I'm perfectly capable of fetching things on my own."

There was no sense in debating that, so he asked, "Is it broken?"

"I'm not sure," Mom replied with a frown. "X-rays are the only way to know, but she refuses to go to the hospital."

"I'm not leaving Will," Gram insisted stubbornly.

This brought to mind why he hated playing chess. He always got into some kind of standoff with his opponent, and he couldn't come up with a way to get out of it. But this was real life, and he couldn't throw in the towel just because things had gotten dicey. Then he had a brainstorm, and he prayed it would work. "Then we'll bring him with us. Where's that wheelchair?"

Gram sent a worried look into the dining room,

and Jason took advantage of her distraction to wink at his mother. Her raised eyebrow told him she understood, and he kept his expression neutral when his grandmother's eyes settled back on him. When they narrowed, he knew she was onto him, but at least she nodded.

"All right, you win," she finally agreed. "Who's taking me to the hospital?"

"My truck's already running," he answered, standing to get her a sweater from its hook near the back door. Holding it up so she could slide her uninjured arm into one sleeve, he looped the rest around her and did up the top two buttons to hold it closed. Hoping to lighten the mood a little, he chuckled. "I remember when you used to do this for me, Gram."

"Now I'd need a ladder," she responded with a fond smile. "Hand me my purse, would you?"

"No, but I'll carry it for you." Dangling the strap over his forearm, he held the other one out for her. "Ready?"

"I suppose. The sooner we leave, the sooner we'll be back."

"That's my girl," he approved heartily. Her ability to cope with bad situations never failed to amaze him.

"I'll keep an eye on Will and have lunch ready when you get back," Mom promised, patting his shoulder while they passed by. "If you need me for anything, just call."

After very carefully helping his grandmother into his truck, Jason got in beside her and drove the ten miles to the hospital in nearby Cambridge as smoothly as possible. The emergency-room nurse was a plump woman with dark, sparkling eyes and a Christmas tree pin on her smock that blinked with multicolored lights.

Tsking with sympathy, she gently guided Gram toward an exam room. "You come with me, honey, and we'll get you fixed up in a blink."

Since she was already in their computer system, all Jason had to do was confirm nothing had changed since they'd treated Gram for pneumonia earlier in the year. After that, he slumped in a waiting-room chair and finally released the iron grip he'd kept on his emotions. It was how he handled a crisis, and it worked well until things settled down and he had a chance to come to terms with what had happened.

As a family, the Barretts had all learned to live with the constant threat of a health issue with Granddad. When you loved someone who had terminal cancer, that kind of acceptance came with the territory. But a problem with Gram was something else entirely.

Their family orbited around her like the sun, and if anything happened to her, Jason feared Granddad wouldn't be physically strong enough to survive her loss.

She's fine, he told himself sternly. *It's only her wrist.* His next thought flipped to Rachel, who'd surely call him in a panic when she went into labor. She had no one else to turn to, and while she and her baby weren't technically his responsibility, he'd already decided that when the time came, he'd be there for them. That trip would be a hundred times more stressful than this one, he knew. Was he ready for it?

Suddenly, he was exhausted, and he bent over, dangling his arms over his knees while he stared at the speckled tiles on the floor. Footsteps hurried toward him, and he lifted his head to find himself gazing into Amy's worried eyes.

"Is your grandmother okay?"

"They're doing X-rays soon, so we'll know more then. How'd you know I was here?"

"Your mom called me," she explained as she took the seat beside him. "She didn't want you here by yourself, pacing and hounding the nurses for information they don't have."

He'd been about five minutes from doing just that, he realized, and he marveled at how well Mom knew him. "That was nice of her, but I hate to drag you over here. Don't you have your Ballet Tots class at noon?"

"I canceled it. We'll make it up later in the week, or they can get a refund for the day. This is much more important." Reaching over, she rested one of her delicate hands over his much larger one. "On the way here, I said a prayer for Olivia to be okay."

Knowing how she'd felt about God not long ago, her revelation astounded him, and he turned to face her. "You did?"

"I'm not sure it will help," she confided, "but it felt like the right thing to do."

"It was," he agreed with heartfelt gratitude. "Thank you."

Suddenly, she seemed uncomfortable, as if her gesture had surprised her as much as it did him. "Can I get you anything?"

Settling his arm across the back of the couch, he gave her shoulders a light bump. "This works for me."

"Well, you'll be hungry soon. There's a deli down the street, so let me know what you want, and I'll get it for you."

"That'd be great. We ate here a lot when Granddad was a patient, and the cafeteria's not the best."

"They never are," she agreed with a grimace. "The hospital I was in after my accident would make a good weight-loss camp. Mom smuggled real food in to me, or I would have starved."

"Sounds pretty awful."

"Don't get me wrong—everyone on the staff was fantastic. I still hated every second of it, not being able to sleep, having people tell me what to do all the time. I wasn't crazy about having to move back in with Mom while I rehabbed, but at least she didn't expect me to be a cheerful patient."

"After what you went through, it must be tough for you to be here," he said gently. "I really appreciate you coming to keep me company, but if you want to go, I'll understand."

"You've done so much for me, and I thought this would be a good way to start repaying you. I'll hang around until Olivia's ready to leave."

"I didn't sign on to the show to make you feel like you owe me something," he argued. "I wanted to help."

She rewarded him with a brilliant smile. "I know that, Galahad. That's why I'm staying."

With that, she snuggled a little closer and rested her head against his shoulder. He wasn't in the mood to talk, and he appreciated her allowing him to sit there in silence. Most women he knew felt compelled to fill every silence longer than three seconds, but not Amy. She seemed to understand that he needed to focus all his energy on absorbing what had happened during what should have been a busy but ordinary day.

Instead, he felt as if it had gone on forever, and it wasn't even lunchtime. Considering what could have happened, Gram had gotten off lightly, and he thanked

God for watching over her. Just having Amy there made things look brighter, he realized. Accustomed to fending for himself since leaving home, he hadn't had anyone to lean on. Even when he and Rachel were together, he'd been the one to take care of everything.

Despite the rocky start he'd gotten, he'd been raised by a family of strong, loyal people who supported each other through every conceivable peak and valley life could throw at them. Paul and Chelsea were the next generation in the Barrett chain, and he'd watched them with growing respect while they built their future with hard work and love.

Rachel's betrayal had soured him on making that same commitment himself, but now he was beginning to think that with the right woman, he could have the kind of relationship he longed for. The kind where two people took on life together and made the best of what God handed them. Over time, he'd realized his mistake with Rachel had been to treat her like a doll, keeping her on a pedestal while he handled everything himself.

He'd never even consider doing that with Amy, and if he went astray, he had no doubt she'd jerk him back into line. And very clearly warn him never to do it again. The thought of it amused him, and in the middle of that sterile waiting room, he couldn't keep back a smile.

He and Amy might look like two mismatched socks, but in his gut he knew that no matter what happened down the road, pairing up with her would be a decision he'd never regret.

Chapter Nine

Amy left Jason and his grandmother in the hospital parking lot with hugs and a promise to check in with them later. As she drove back to Arabesque, she mulled over what had gone on and what it meant.

Mostly, she tried to analyze what had compelled her to appeal to the God she'd been so angry with. Jason had clearly been stunned by it, and she could relate to how he felt. Maybe attending services with him and singing all those uplifting Christmas hymns had mellowed her attitude, chipping away at the grudge she'd carried for so long. Whatever the explanation, she couldn't deny feeling liberated, as if a huge weight had been taken from her.

Even more surprising, throughout the afternoon, that light feeling stayed with her. To her, that meant it wasn't a fluke or some lingering effect from an emergency situation that had turned out well. It was sticking because it was real. Understanding settled in, and as she cued up her favorite section of *The Nutcracker* score on the studio's sound system, she glanced up with a smile. "Thank you."

A warm softness brushed her cheek, as if someone had reached down to reassure her. Tears sprang into her eyes, and she resolutely blinked them away but held on to the emotion they evoked in her heart. It was comforting to know someone was watching over her, even when she thought she was alone.

Jason and Brenda were right, she finally admitted to herself. God had never deserted her, but had seen her on the wrong path and manipulated her circumstances to correct her direction. That fateful course shift had brought her to Barrett's Mill and a man who could see beyond her imperfections to who she truly was.

Suddenly anxious to hear Jason's voice, she thumbed through her contacts list and chose his number. While she waited for him to answer, she impulsively added him to her very short speed-dial list. It was only for people she spoke to frequently, and since they talked at least twice a day, she figured he belonged there.

After a few rings, he picked up. "Hey there. What's up?"

From the background noise, she knew he was at the mill. She didn't think now was the right time to share her epiphany, so she kept things light. "Checking in, as promised. How's Olivia doing?"

"Home with Mom and Granddad. Gram's supposed to be resting, but I hear she's trying to come up with a way to make dinner one-handed."

"Can't your mother take care of that?"

He let out a tired-sounding laugh. "Sure, but that's not how it works in Gram's kitchen. She's in charge, and everyone else assists. I think that's where Paul got his bossy gene from."

"I heard that," his brother chimed in from a distance. "Are you assembling that rocking chair or flirting?"

"Both."

Paul groaned, and Amy interpreted the sound of a slamming door as her cue to finish up. "You're busy, so I'll let you go."

"I've got three more of these rockers to do, but I'll be in after rehearsal to paint that marble detail on the fireplace."

"Why don't you just go home after work?" she suggested. "The painting can wait another day."

"Are you sure? That'll put us off your schedule."

Her schedule, she echoed ruefully. After the long, trying day he'd had, he was willing to stretch it even further to keep her happy. She hated the idea that her inflexibility was putting more pressure on this kind, compassionate man. After all, what was the worst that could happen? Certainly not anything that warranted him wearing himself out during the holidays. "We'll get it done. If we really get in a jam, I'll ask Jenna to come help us out."

"Oh, man," he groaned. "Don't do that. She'd never let me hear the end of it."

"Everyone needs a hand now and then. Even big, strong lumberjacks like you."

"I'll finish those sets myself if it kills me," he assured her. "I made a commitment to you, and I never go back on my word."

Amy was more than a little impressed. She'd given him an out, but he stubbornly refused to take it. Most people she knew were quick to choose the path of least resistance, but not this one. Even though he had a perfectly viable excuse, she trusted him to deliver exactly what he'd promised her, in time for their show. That was the kind of guy every girl needed in her life, she mused with a smile. The kind who stood up and took his responsibilities seriously instead of dodging them at the first sign of trouble.

"All right, but I'm willing to help if you tell me what you need." The line went quiet, and after a few seconds she said, "Jason?"

"Yeah, I'm here."

"Is something wrong?"

"No, it's just—" Heaving a sigh, he went on. "I guess I'm more tired than I thought is all. I'll see you tomorrow."

Something in his voice sounded off, but she couldn't quite peg it, so she accepted his explanation. After all, he'd been through a lot today. She'd experienced enough of that herself to understand how draining it could be. "Have a good night."

"You, too."

She'd no sooner hung up than her phone rang again. Checking the caller ID, she was surprised to see it was the doctor who'd led the surgical team that operated on her after her accident. They hadn't been in touch recently, and she couldn't imagine what he wanted. "Hello, Dr. Fitzgerald. How are you?"

"Excited," he replied in his usual brisk way. "I think you will be, too, when you hear what I have to say."

Amy felt her pulse spike, then cautioned herself to remain calm. Her hopes had been raised many times in the past, only to be dashed later on. Steadying her voice, she said, "Go ahead."

In a tone laced with more of the same enthusiasm, he described an experimental procedure he and some colleagues had developed for treating injuries like hers. Their initial trials had gone well, and they were looking for volunteers to undergo the treatment for real.

"Based on your age and general health," he continued, "I think you'd be an excellent candidate."

"Why haven't I heard about this on the news?" she asked warily.

"It's experimental, and we don't want to publicize it until we have some solid results to report. I have to warn you, there is a potential downside."

Of course there was, she groused silently. There was always a downside. "I'm listening."

"If it's successful, this surgery should restore your full range of motion through your back and legs."

"And if it fails?"

"You could be paralyzed."

Could be, she echoed silently. Two tantalizing words she'd heard so often, clinging to the slender hope that somehow her body would find a way to heal itself and function the way it was supposed to. But that hadn't happened, and she wasn't certain she could muster the emotional energy to risk suffering through that kind of disappointment again.

Still, the idea of walking freely—maybe even dancing again—was incredibly tempting. She wasn't foolish enough to think she'd ever be a prima ballerina. That dream had died long ago, but she might be able to take on secondary roles in a small company somewhere. It wasn't her ideal, but at least that way she'd be doing what she loved.

"I'll have to think about it," she finally said. "When do you need my answer?"

"Tomorrow, at the latest. One of our original volunteers opted out, and we have to fill the spot quickly to keep everything on track. We've reserved a section of the hospital for our patients, and we need to do quite a bit of prep work beforehand. You'd need to be here in New York right after Christmas, and the actual procedure would be done in early January. If you decide you're not interested, I have to start going down my list and find someone else."

Oh, she was interested, all right. The timing would allow her to finish up *The Nutcracker* and spend time with her family before leaving for New York. Since her mother was coming for the show, she'd catch a ride back with her and be able to stay at her Manhattan apartment following her surgery.

Was she really considering this? While her mind clicked through the things she'd have to do to make this work, it became obvious that part of her was already on board.

Another part, the one she'd only recently begun to discover, whispered a single—but very important—objection.

What about Jason?

Putting aside a question she couldn't easily answer, she wrapped up her call. "I'll definitely get back to you, one way or the other. Whatever I decide, I'm so grateful you thought of me. This is a wonderful opportunity for someone like me."

"We'll talk tomorrow, then. Goodbye, Amy."

She hung up, watching as the wallpaper on her phone's screen faded back into place. It was a picture of Jason and her at the Starlight Festival, gazing upward as the star on top of the town tree was being lit. Chelsea had taken the photo and texted it to her, and it had immediately become Amy's favorite. He stood behind her in the protective way she'd come to associate with him. Although he wasn't touching her, she could almost feel those strong arms wrapped around her, shielding her from the press of the crowd.

It was a comforting sensation she'd come to rely on as their unexpected friendship continued to grow. If she agreed to the surgical trial and it went well, what then? In her heart, she knew that if there was even a sliver of a chance for her to perform again, she wouldn't be content teaching no matter how adorable her students were.

But if it turned out to be another failure, she might never walk again. Then what would she do to support herself? Beyond that, if she was confined to a wheelchair for the rest of her life, her flickering hopes of marriage and adopting a child might be gone forever.

Completely overwhelmed by the choice she was faced with, she did something that not long ago would never have occurred to her. Looking up, she said, "I trust that You brought me to this point for a reason. Please help me do the right thing."

Nothing.

While she hadn't expected an immediate response, some kind of sign would have been nice.

The alert on her phone chimed, reminding her it was almost time for rehearsal. As if on cue, the front door jingled and high-pitched voices blended with the classical Christmas music she'd left playing in the studio.

Her answer would have to wait, she supposed as she stood to meet her early arrivals. Because if this turned out to be her final *Nutcracker* production, she was determined to give it everything she had.

* * *

"It's me!" Jason hollered on his way into Arabesque the following day. "Don't shoot!"

Amy was onstage adjusting the long drapes that hung around the fake bay window in the ballroom. When she turned to look at him, his heart rolled over in his chest like a lovesick hound. Even though he'd been engaged before, this sensation was like nothing he'd ever felt, and he wasn't sure what to make of it. He'd just seen Amy yesterday, but it felt as if it had been much longer.

Oh, man, he thought with a mental groan. Somehow, when he wasn't paying attention, he'd stumbled into some dangerous territory. It was one thing to admire a pretty girl, but for a guy like him who'd been dropped hard, doing emotional cartwheels wasn't smart. If only he knew how to stop.

"Hi there," Amy said when she met him in the wings. "How's Olivia today?"

"Better, I think. She never complains about anything, so it's hard to tell."

"I wish more people were like that," Amy commented wryly.

"Tell me about it." Setting down his toolbox, he mentally reviewed where they were on her list. "So tonight, it's the bookcases and fireplace, right?"

"Jason, we need to talk."

Not what he wanted to hear. Those were troublemaker words every man dreaded, and he braced himself for the worst. "Okay."

"I'm sorry," she began, twisting her hands in obvious distress. "I didn't mean to jump into it like that. Would you like a snack or something?"

"No, I'm good." She looked so upset, he wanted noth-

ing more than to chase away whatever was bothering
her. Even if it turned out to be him. Taking a seat on the
steps leading down from the stage, he patted the one
above him. She hesitated, but finally sat down, and he
gave her an encouraging nod. "Go ahead."

Another pause, then she plunged right in. "One of
the surgeons who operated on me after my accident
called me. He and some of his colleagues have developed a new procedure that could restore my full range
of motion."

"Amy, that's awesome!" When she frowned, he felt
his expression fall to mirror hers. "It's not awesome?"

"It could be," she allowed, avoiding his gaze while
she picked at a stray piece of tape on the stage. "But if
it doesn't work, I could end up being paralyzed."

For a few seconds, Jason was so stunned he couldn't
think of a single thing to say. When his brain began
functioning on all cylinders again, he understood why
she was so skittish about sharing her news with him.
"You're seriously thinking about doing this, aren't you?"

"Yes."

She didn't say anything more, but when her eyes met
his, the defiance glittering in them spoke for her. She
wasn't asking for his opinion, he realized, or his per-
mission. But he couldn't stand by and watch her risk
her health this way. "I think it's a bad idea."

"I didn't ask you."

"That doesn't mean I don't have a few thoughts on
the subject."

Jumping up, he began pacing in front of the huge
Christmas tree they and the kids had decorated for the
show. He'd lifted Clara up to place the star on top, and
like a moron he'd envisioned doing that with his own lit-

tle girl someday. The memory surfaced from nowhere, and he firmly pushed it back down to wherever it had come from.

Staring up at the pulleys and cables that operated the stage curtains, he closed his eyes and sent up a fervent prayer for patience. When he felt calmer, he turned to face Amy. "Please explain to me why you're considering this."

"Because it could be my last chance to fix what's wrong with me."

That was the root of the problem, he understood. Her obsession with perfection had bothered him in the past, but never more than in this moment. Because he'd always been aware of his own failings, he couldn't comprehend her perspective on what it meant to be flawless. But he did understand that in the past she'd been just that, and she longed to reclaim as much of it as she could.

That didn't mean he couldn't try to change her mind, though.

"There's nothing wrong with you," he insisted, crossing the stage to hunker down in front of her. "You're perfect just the way you are."

Her wistful gaze communicated more than any words could possibly say. "That's sweet of you, but we both know it isn't true."

Taking her hand, he met those sorrow-filled blue eyes with every ounce of compassion he had in him. "I believe it is, with all my heart."

"Please don't take this the wrong way," she begged in a tearful voice. "But that doesn't really matter. What matters is what *I* believe."

Since he shared that particular conviction with her,

he had no choice but to give her that one. Thankfully, another argument floated into his mind. "Okay, so what'll you do if the surgery goes wrong and you're paralyzed? It's hard to teach dance when you can't show the kids the steps."

"I'll find another job somewhere."

He could tell she was trying desperately to appear confident, but the shadow of doubt in her expressive eyes gave her away. The only thing she'd ever wanted to do was dance, or teach dance, so he was fairly certain she'd never learned how to do anything else. It was mean of him, but he forged ahead in what he suspected would be a last-ditch attempt to make her see reason. "Doing what?"

"I don't know, something," she retorted defiantly. "Rachel's not exactly a rocket scientist. If she can find a job, so can I."

The uncalled-for attack on his ex made Jason's temper flare, and he wrestled it under control to keep this from getting personal. He couldn't accomplish anything if he lost his cool and started yelling. "We're not talking about her right now. We're talking about you. What's really bothering you?"

At first, Amy just glowered at him, which worked in his favor because it gave him a chance to rein his own emotions back into line. She meant a lot to him, and he wanted nothing more than for her to be happy. This just didn't seem to him like the smartest way to go about it, but Granddad had taught him that the best way to resolve a disagreement was to listen to the other side all the way through. And since this was such a huge decision for Amy, Jason figured he owed her that much.

"This is very important to me," she finally said, her

voice trembling with a mixture of anger and disappointment. "I thought you'd be more supportive than—"

She cut off abruptly, but it didn't take a genius to fill in that blank.

"Devon?" This time, he didn't bother hiding his frustration and stood to his full height. As he folded his arms in his most intimidating pose, it was his turn to scowl. "You're seriously gonna compare me to that snake?"

"He always told me what I should do," she argued, "how I should handle my career. You're doing the same thing now, trying to talk me out of having this surgery."

"Because it could ruin your life!"

"It's my life, and I have no intention of letting someone else talk me into anything."

She tilted her chin rebelliously, and he recognized that he was treading on extremely thin ice with her. She was a grown woman, and ordinarily he'd honor her right to choose the option she felt was best for her. But what she was contemplating made absolutely no sense to him. Beyond that, she'd come so far in making a new career here in Barrett's Mill. Whatever the outcome of her surgery, he feared she'd eventually regret leaving the studio for the slim possibility of reviving her performing career.

"What about your students?" he demanded. "I thought you liked working with them."

"I love it," she affirmed in a wistful tone. "But there's no way for me to have that and my own career besides."

Sensing that she was wavering, he took a single step forward into the space he normally kept between them. The urge to hold her was so overwhelming, it took some serious willpower to keep his hands at his sides. Very quietly, he said, "That's a tough choice to make."

"I know."

She looked up at him with such longing, he almost couldn't stand it. Part of him wanted to jump in and offer to go with her, even if only until her surgery was complete and she knew the outcome. Once the holidays were over, things would slow down at the mill enough to allow him to take some time off. Then logic reasserted itself to remind him he was a country boy who'd be completely lost in the big city.

It killed him to admit that, but he couldn't deceive her. Or himself. He might give that life a shot to please her, but he'd visited enough busy places to know that in the long run he'd never last. They were too crowded, and the hectic lifestyle made him long for wide-open spaces where he could breathe. Amy fit nicely into Barrett's Mill, but he couldn't envision himself doing the same in a bustling place like New York.

Because of that, if they were going to remain together, she was the one who had to compromise. Which meant he had to come up with a way to convince her to stay. "What happens to the studio if you leave?"

"Aunt Helen will finish out this block of classes and then close it down. That was her plan before I came here, anyway."

"It's a shame to disappoint all those kids," he ventured, hoping to appeal to her affection for the children she'd come to like so much.

"There's a good teacher over in Cambridge. I'm sure she'll be happy to take them on."

"She's not you." *In so many ways,* he added silently.

"I don't expect you to understand," she said, backing away from him in an unmistakable effort to put some distance between them. "But this could be my last chance at being the way I used to be. I have to take it."

He'd tried every trick in his book, knowing all the while how it would end. When Amy set her mind on something, there was simply no budging her. Grudgingly, he gave in. "Like you said, it's your life."

"Yes, it is." Glancing around, she came back to him with the same detached look in her eyes he'd seen the first day he met her. "I think the sets are far enough along that Uncle Fred and I can finish them up. Thank you so much for all your help, Jason."

Offering her hand, she stared at him with an unreadable expression. Now that he'd voiced an opinion that differed from hers, apparently he'd slid down the list from good friend to hired hand. Must be some kind of record, he groused as he politely shook her hand. There were so many things he wanted to tell her, but he knew they'd sound either lame or pathetic or both, so he kept them to himself. "You're welcome."

Since there was really nothing more to say, he picked up his toolbox and headed for the door. The bells jingled, a cheerful sound at odds with the heaviness weighing him down as he left. He knew he should just keep going, but he couldn't help looking back. What he saw just about broke his heart.

Standing alone in the middle of the ballroom, framed in the halo of a spotlight, Amy was staring up at the star on top of the lighted tree. The scene brought to mind their evening at the Starlight Festival, when they'd confided in each other and started building something that had become much more than friendship for him. The little ballerina he'd admired as a child had grown into an exquisite, aggravating woman who had an uncanny ability to challenge him one moment and charm him the next. Watching her now, he wished there was something more he could do to persuade her to rethink her decision and stay. Since there wasn't, he turned and headed for home.

On his way, he passed by the Morgan house. The lights were in in Fred's garage workshop, and Jason impulsively switched direction. As he approached, he could hear smooth jazz music, and he grinned when he heard Fred mimicking a soulful high-range trumpet solo with considerable gusto.

Outside the partially open door, he knocked to get the mechanic's attention. Fred appeared surprised to see him, but waved him in. When his eyes locked on Jason's toolbox, he scowled. "Those sets aren't near done yet. What happened?"

"Amy fired me."

Heaving a long-suffering male sigh, Fred pulled up a couple of apple crates and motioned for Jason to take one. Once they were seated, he fixed Jason with a woe-begone look. "The women in this family can drive a man right off a cliff."

"Got that right," Jason growled back.

Amy's uncle listened patiently to the entire sad story, nodding and frowning in all the right places.

"I've never been booted in the middle of a job before," Jason said. "She'd rather have you help her finish things up before the show next week."

"No can do." Holding his lower back, Fred winked. "I think I tweaked my lumbar again."

They both laughed, and Jason appreciated the conniving support. "Whattaya think I should do?"

"Ignore her and finish what you started." Taking

out his key ring, he slid one off and handed it to Jason. "This way, she doesn't have to let you in."

"Thanks." Pocketing the key, he added, "Now, about the other thing."

Scratching a thumb over his stubbly chin, the older man chewed on that one for a few seconds. "Well, now, that depends on what you're really after."

"I'm not following you."

"Women are complicated."

Jason snorted his agreement. "Tell me about it."

"What I mean is it's best to pick one thing and go full bore instead of spreading yourself too thin." Jason didn't respond, and he continued, "Do you want her to stay here so you can see where things go with her, or pass on the surgery 'cause you think it's a mistake?"

"Both."

Chuckling, Fred shook his head. "You're not listening, son. To you and me, those two things are one and the same. To Amy, they're completely different."

At first, that made no sense to him. Then he reconsidered it from her perspective, and the pieces clicked into place. "Because one's professional and the other's personal. If you don't mind me asking, where do you and Helen stand on this experimental procedure?"

"Against, one thousand percent. But Amy and that headstrong baby sister of mine have got other ideas. I guess Connie sees it different than we do, 'cause when she was younger, she was planning to be a big-time ballerina herself."

"Then she had Amy," Jason guessed, getting a nod in reply. "That explains why Amy's dead set on getting back to it. Her mom missed out, so Amy's trying to make up for what she lost."

"Don't get me wrong. From the time she could walk, Amy danced the way most of us breathe, and that car crash was a tragedy in more ways than one. It wasn't easy for her to dust herself off the way she's done, but she's making the most of the gifts God gave her."

"I thought she felt that way, too," Jason confided glumly. "Now I'm not so sure. She seems to love teaching those kids, but now she's ready to give all that up for something even the doctors are warning her might not work."

"You're not seeing it from her angle. If you'd fallen out of a tree in Oregon a couple years ago and were done with logging, what would you have done?"

"Come back here and make furniture at the mill." That got him a wise look, but he didn't understand the significance of his answer. Eventually, it dawned on him. "I get it. I chose that even when I didn't have to. Amy took over the studio because that was the only way she could still be involved in dancing."

"Now you've got it." With a suddenly somber look, Fred asked, "And what about the other thing?"

Jason blanked, then caught on and grinned. "Are you asking about my intentions toward your niece?"

"Yes, I am."

Since there were all manner of tools only an arm's length away, Jason straightened up and looked him directly in the eye the way he'd been taught. "She's the most incredible woman I've ever met, and I'd love to get to know her better."

Fred seemed to appreciate that, and he nodded his approval. "From what I see, you're a good influence on our girl. She's a mite serious for someone her age, and you lighten her up. She smiles a lot more these days, and I like that."

"That's good to hear."

"But." Brandishing a heavy wrench that looked as if it had seen plenty of action, he warned, "If that ever changes, you and I are gonna have a problem. Understand?"

Jason nodded soberly. "Yes, sir."

"Good boy. Now, get outta here so I can finish up before Helen starts yelling for me to come inside already."

Figuring it was best to get while the getting was good, Jason retrieved his toolbox and made a quick exit. While he mulled over Fred's advice, he had to admit he was having a tough time letting Amy go the way she wanted him to. He'd never had trouble doing that before, so his newfound reluctance puzzled him. Even with Rachel, once he'd gotten over the initial shock of her bolting like that, he'd counted his blessings that she'd skated before they'd walked down the aisle. Afterward would've been a lot tougher for him to recover from.

Amy was a different story.

She always had been, he realized with a start. As a boy, he'd been awed by her, and when they reconnected as adults, he just picked up where he'd left off. He didn't recall many things from that time in his life, but he'd never forgotten the spritely ballerina with the sparkling eyes and dazzling smile.

Had she remained in his memory all these years for a reason? He'd always believed that God created a match for everyone, and he couldn't deny it was possible Amy was meant to be his. The kicker was, if a relationship between them was ever going to work, one of them would have to do some pretzel-style bending of a fairly strong will.

He wasn't prepared to make that kind of life-altering concession, and Amy had made it clear she wasn't, either. So where did that leave them? His thoughts spiraled downward from there, and by the time he reached his grandparents' house, he was as discouraged as he'd ever been in his life.

As if Granddad's worsening illness wasn't enough, now Jason could add losing Amy to the list. Hands down, this was going to be the worst Christmas ever.

Chapter Ten

After stewing for a while, Amy came to the conclusion that she'd unfairly pummeled Jason with months' worth of frustration and resentment. And God bless him, he'd stood there and taken every blow without either retaliating or backing down. He'd held his ground, making it abundantly clear he was doing it for her own good. She wasn't accustomed to fighting so vigorously with someone and not coming out the winner.

Unfortunately, this time she might have won the argument, but she'd lost the respect of someone who'd come to mean more to her than she'd fully realized until now. Truth be told, Jason had pinpointed some of her reservations so accurately, it had frightened her. And when she was scared, she puffed herself up like a threatened kitten and lashed out with her claws. It wasn't pretty, and she wasn't proud of it, but there it was. He'd treated her with nothing other than kindness and care, and she'd rewarded him with venom.

At the very least, she owed him an apology. The humble-pie kind best delivered in person. A quick glance at the clock showed her it was still relatively early, and she had plenty of time to go to choir rehearsal, stammer her regret and slink into her usual place in the soprano section.

She knew it was best to get things like this over with, so she pushed away from her desk and reluctantly headed for the front door. The night air was cool but pleasant, and it felt good on her face. The view of Christmas lights and decorations up and down Main Street lifted her spirits considerably, and by the time she reached the Crossroads Church, she felt slightly better about talking with Jason.

He was the most patient, tolerant man she'd ever met, she reassured herself as she climbed the steps. Now that the dust had settled, he must understand how important this opportunity was to her. She only hoped he'd be able to forgive her cold behavior and they could remain friends. Because she had to admit, the shy little girl who still lived inside her adored the burly lumberjack with the generous heart. Perhaps, if they stayed in touch, their paths would intersect again and...

What? Pausing in the vestibule, she took a moment to let that thought play out. Unfortunately, it dead-ended right there, leaving her with a big, unanswered question echoing in her mind. Did she want more than friendship with Jason? Even if she did, he might not feel the same. And if he shared her feelings, how on earth would they make a serious relationship work? Soon, it would be more than distance separating them. She was as driven as he was easygoing, and she'd probably make him nuts within a month.

Then again, she reasoned as she went into the chapel, they'd been working together at the studio all this time and after getting accustomed to each other's vastly different styles, they'd proven to be an excellent team. Then there were those promising kisses under the mistletoe. She wouldn't mind some more of those. The trouble was, she'd learned the hard way that things didn't always go the way she wanted them to. If a romance with Jason went awry, she'd lose him altogether. She didn't even want to consider that.

Left with a thorny problem and no concrete solution, she took her spot next to Brenda and greeted the other singers around her. Jason wasn't there yet, so she distracted herself by admiring the decorations the Ladies' Aid had brought in.

Evergreen ropes were swagged all around the little church, and each windowsill held a rich burgundy poinsettia and an electric candle. On either side of the altar stood a tall tree, decorated in tasteful white lights and velvet ribbons. Each had a crystal star at the top that caught the light, tossing prisms onto the old wooden floorboards. Simple elegance, she thought with a smile. She couldn't imagine a more fitting way to deck out this charming country chapel nestled in the Blue Ridge valley.

Mrs. Griggs called for their attention, and everyone quieted down. A quick glance over at the tenors showed Amy that Jason still hadn't arrived, and she frowned. As he'd so emphatically told her, he didn't duck his responsibilities, and she worried that something might have happened.

Leaning in, she asked Brenda, "Is everything all right with the Barretts?"

"As far as I know," she whispered back. "If it wasn't, Mom would've heard about it and told us."

Amy didn't doubt that for a second, and as the soprano line picked up their part in "O Holy Night," she decided Jason must be working late to finish one of his many projects at the mill. Christmas was coming up fast, and furniture orders had to be shipped soon to arrive on time. Reassured, she put him out of her mind and focused on accurately hitting as many of the notes as she could.

As a dancer, she'd spent most of her holidays onstage, so the prospect of a Christmas Eve performance was nothing new for her. But back then, she'd been one of the stars, not part of a large group like this. The camaraderie was a novel experience, and she found herself enjoying it more than she'd anticipated.

Much of the time she'd spent back in her hometown had been like that, she realized with a smile. She couldn't recall being this content anywhere else, and she knew Jason had a lot to do with that. With his thoughtful, attentive nature, he'd helped to heal old wounds she hadn't been aware she was still carrying. She only hoped the rest of her stay here would be just as happy.

Before she knew it, rehearsal was over. Mrs. Griggs reminded them all that next week would be their last practice, and they should plan on arriving early Christmas Eve to warm up their voices and do a few run-throughs before the service began.

Eager to put her apology behind her, Amy stopped outside and brought up Jason's number from her list. When he didn't answer, she assumed he was in the noisy workshop and couldn't hear his phone. She wanted to speak to him in person, so she opted not to leave a message. That way, he'd see he missed a call from her and could return it if he wanted to talk to her.

If he didn't…well, at least then she'd know where

she stood with him. After the way she'd behaved, she didn't deserve his forgiveness, but she prayed he'd give it to her anyway.

Strolling up the sidewalk toward Arabesque, she noticed a subdued glow in the front window. She'd deliberately left the outside display on, but the studio itself had been dark when she left. Then it occurred to her that Jason must have told Uncle Fred he was going to have to finish the sets for the show. She felt horrible for imposing on a man still nursing an injured back, but she really had no choice.

Hoping to make things easier on him, she picked up her pace and mentally prepared herself to be as helpful as her meager carpentry skills would allow. She unlocked the front door, quieting the bells while she closed it and turned the dead bolt behind her. When she caught the sound of classic rock coming from the stage, she looked over in surprise.

There was Jason, a paintbrush in either hand, applying the faux marble finish she'd chosen for the fireplace. Normally, he looked happy while he was working, but tonight he wore a grim expression, as if he was putting in his time and couldn't wait to leave. That was her fault, but the upside was that since she'd done it, she was the one person who could undo it.

Before she had a chance to reconsider, she walked through the wings and paused behind him. He didn't acknowledge her presence in any way, and she swallowed hard before saying, "That looks really nice."

"It's what you said you wanted," he said, not looking at her as he continued painting. "I'm just following orders."

Flat and emotionless, somehow his words still had

a bite to them. At first, she didn't understand why, but she quickly figured it out. Jason always spoke to her with warmth in his voice and a twinkle in his eyes. While she knew the cold shoulder was well deserved, she couldn't bear communicating with him this way. "Could you stop for a minute?"

"I have to keep blending or the paint'll dry the wrong color."

"I don't care."

Pausing midstroke, he angled a look back at her. "Seriously? I thought everything had to be perfect for the show."

"It will be." Hearing the confidence in her tone, she realized she truly meant what she'd said. "You'll make it perfect, because that's what you do."

Setting the brushes across the top of an open can, he stood and faced her. "I try."

"I know you do," she assured him quickly. "Jason, please forgive me for the way I acted yesterday. I was feeling overwhelmed, and I took it out on you. That wasn't fair, and neither was comparing you to Devon. You're nothing like him, and it was wrong of me to accuse you of being otherwise."

Gazing down at her, his eyes shone with compassion. "You're scared about the surgery, aren't you?"

"Terrified," she confirmed on a shaky breath. "But I'm more scared of not giving it a chance. I mean, what if it works?"

"What if it doesn't?"

"That's the problem," she agreed solemnly. "I've never had to make a huge decision like this that could mess up the rest of my life. One minute, I'm sure going ahead with the procedure is the right thing for me, and the next I want to call Dr. Fitzgerald and back out. I'm so confused, it's like I'm spinning in circles."

Grasping one of her hands, he reeled her into his arms and held her tightly against his chest. With his heart beating a steady cadence under her cheek, Amy felt as if nothing in the world could possibly harm her. Part of her wanted nothing more than to stay right where she was, but the tug of a dream left unfulfilled was pulling her in another direction.

Tipping her head back, she gazed up at the man who'd done so much for her. He'd brought the very best part of her back to life, and the thought of leaving him behind was almost more than she could stand.

Cupping her cheek in his callused hand, he leaned in to brush a gentle kiss over her lips. Then he rested his forehead against hers and sighed. "This surgery is really what you want?"

The acceptance in his tone, despite the misgivings he'd so loudly stated, touched her deeply. "Yes, but I'm still petrified."

"That's 'cause you're a smart cookie." He ticked the tip of her nose with his finger. "But if it doesn't work, I hope you know there's always a place for you here in Barrett's Mill."

"With you?" The words slipped out on their own, and she felt her face reddening in embarrassment. When would she learn to think first and blurt later?

Thankfully, Jason met her slipup with a chuckle. "Well, I'm not going anywhere."

It wasn't a yes, but it wasn't a no, either. Normally, she detested getting a wishy-washy maybe, but considering the circumstances, she'd have to take what he was willing to offer her. For now, it was enough to know he didn't hate her and would support her decision, even though he didn't understand it.

Some days, that was the best a girl could hope for.

"There's my girl!" Stepping out of a rented convertible, Connie Morgan all but smothered Amy in an enthusiastic hug. Eyeing her critically, she smiled. "You look wonderful. I wasn't sure you'd like it here after so many years away, but it seems to agree with you."

"Aunt Helen and Uncle Fred have been taking good care of me," Amy replied with a smile of her own. "And it's fun getting to hang out with Brenda again. She always was my favorite cousin."

"Oh, I remember you two when you were little. Always whispering and giggling about one thing or another."

"It's pretty much the same now," Amy told her. "It's just now we talk about her kids instead of all the cool new clothes we want for our Barbies."

"How fun." With an arm still around her shoulders, Mom turned to look at the front of the studio. Amy had left all the decorative lights on, and in the cloudy morning the effect was pretty much the same as at night. "Just beautiful. I especially like the arbor and the tree with all those twinkling lights. They really capture the whimsy of *The Nutcracker*."

"Have you been reading Broadway reviews again?" Amy teased, hugging her mother back. "I'm glad you like it, but I had a lot of help."

"Jason," Mom said with a knowing look. "I've heard a lot about him, but not from you. I wonder why that is."

A blush crept over Amy's cheeks, and she hedged,

"I figured Aunt Helen would tell you everything you needed to know."

"Hometown boy, back from the wilds of Oregon to help save his family's business and yours, besides. He sounds like a hero straight out of a romantic movie."

Amy couldn't agree more, but she hesitated to voice her opinion of him and give her mother the wrong idea. Her relationship with Jason was tentative, at best, and she wasn't at all certain how it would end. Her family had been through so much since her accident, she didn't want to drag them through any more drama.

Then she noticed a familiar green pickup coming up Main Street, and she realized her plan was about to be blown apart. Once her mother saw her with Jason, she'd have to fess up and admit she felt more than friendship for the tall lumberjack. A lot more.

"Is that him?" Mom asked.

"Yes. Please behave yourself."

"Why would you—" He stepped from the cab, and Mom let out a sigh of approval. "Oh, my."

Amy couldn't help grinning, because she felt the same way as he strode toward them. Strong and solid, he moved with an innate confidence that made other men look small by comparison. "Mother, try to remember he's my age."

"Oh, sweetie, I'm just looking," she said airily, then giggled. "And admiring."

"All the girls around here do."

"Do what?" Jason asked as he joined them.

"Think you're a hunk," Amy replied, laughing when he made a face. Resting a hand on her mother's shoulder, she went on. "Jason Barrett, this is my mom, Connie Morgan."

"Pleased to meet you, ma'am," he said, shaking her hand gently. "I have to say, this is quite the daughter you've raised. You must be real proud of her."

"Every day." Giving him a chiding look, she warned, "But if you call me 'ma'am' again, we're going to have a serious problem."

"Yes, m—Ms. Morgan," he amended with a quick grin.

"Connie."

"All right, then. If you ladies can swing the door for me, I've got the last of the set pieces in my truck. I painted them last night, so they're dry and ready to put in place."

"Last night?" Amy echoed in disbelief. "You mean, after you worked till eleven at the mill?"

"You needed 'em today."

His casual response made his effort sound like it was nothing, but to her it was a very big deal. No one outside her family had ever gone to such lengths for her. Not to mention, he'd kept on working when she'd specifically—and quite rudely—ordered him to stop. She couldn't envision anyone else doing the same, and that he'd persevered in spite of her was remarkable, to say the least.

Mom had discreetly moved away and was making a good show of checking out Arabesque's charming window display. Amy took advantage of the relative privacy to reward her Galahad with her very best smile.

"Yes, I did." Since they were in full view of anyone on Main Street, she stood on tiptoe to kiss his cheek. "Thank you."

Leaning in, Jason murmured, "If I go in and set 'em up right now, can I get another one of those afterward?"

"I think that could be arranged."

That got him moving, and in no time the *Nutcracker* ballroom was complete. Amy went through the wings to the control panel and hollered, "Stand in the audience area and tell me how everything looks from there."

She dimmed the houselights and flipped all the switches connected to the stage. At first, she didn't hear anything from out front, and she feared something had gone wrong.

Then her mother called out, "Amy, it's absolutely perfect! Come see."

Amy hurried out to join them and was thrilled to see Mom was right. Sneaking an arm around Jason's back, she gave him a quick hug. Smiling up at him, she said, "It *is* perfect, and it's all because of you."

"Well, you gave me a book full of detailed instructions," he teased with a grin. "It's pretty hard to miss when someone lays it all out for you."

"I hope the show goes as well," she confided.

"It will," he commented with a reassuring squeeze. "Just have a little faith."

Not long ago, she'd have tightened up if someone had said that to her. Now that she'd found her way back to her Christian roots, his advice settled warmly over her and made her feel more confident about tomorrow's performance. God had brought her back to her tiny hometown for this, she realized. He knew all along this was where she'd find the man who could accept her as she was and help her overcome the crushing disappointment that had stripped her of her dream.

Barrett's Mill had come to mean more to her than she could have expected when she reluctantly returned to take over the struggling studio. Jason in particular had shown her there were selfless people in the world who did what they thought was best for those they cared about, even when it hurt.

While Jason and Mom chatted about the upcoming show, it struck Amy that she'd become quite attached to this alternate life of hers. While it hadn't been her first choice, she now considered it a good option for her. Teaching came with none of the stress of performing, not to mention she could pretty much eat whatever she wanted. With an aunt whose scrumptious family recipes consistently won blue ribbons, that was an important consideration.

With Jason's arm lightly around her shoulders, she recognized that she had two good lives to pick from. One included him and this close-knit community populated by down-to-earth folks who looked out for each other and pitched in without a second thought. The other was filled with bright lights and excitement, both on-stage and off.

Which was better for her? A few weeks ago, the answer would have been obvious to her, but now she wasn't so sure. Professional success had always taken precedence over her personal life, and she'd been content that way. That was before she met Jason, though, and learned what it meant to step out of the spotlight and just be herself.

Her thoughts were so jumbled, she felt as if she was standing at the juncture of two vastly different paths. Unaccustomed to being confused about the direction she should take, she sent up a quick prayer for guidance. After all, God had gone to a lot of trouble to lead her back here. Certainly, He knew which course was best for her to follow.

Although she knew better than to expect an immediate response, she couldn't deny being a little disappointed not to get some kind of sign. Apparently, as He'd done before, He believed she could handle this one on her own.

If only she could agree with Him.

Jason had never been so nervous.

Peeking around the side of a velvet curtain, he noticed the seating area in front of the stage was even fuller than it had been the last time he checked. At her post near the door, Brenda Lattimore greeted each person brightly, taking their money and handing them one of the parchment tickets Amy had designed and printed herself. Elegant but understated, just like the woman moving through the crowd, welcoming her guests and wishing them a fun afternoon.

As if they could help it, he thought with a grin. The ballroom behind him glowed with the subtle lighting he'd installed, ready to be cranked up to full wattage once the kids were in their places onstage. For now, classical Christmas music was playing quietly over the speakers, and he checked the notes Amy had given him—again—with his cues for switching tracks to Tchaikovsky and when to open and close the curtains.

If he messed this up for her, he'd kick himself until the Fourth of July. Assuming her surgery went the way she hoped, this would be Arabesque's one and only production. While he was usually laid-back about things, this time he wanted everything to be perfect.

He was starting to sound like Amy, he chided himself, taking a deep breath to calm his nerves. After one last glance, he folded the paper and slid it into the inside pocket of his only suit jacket. Then he closed his eyes and pictured the kids taking their bows after a stellar performance, the audience standing and clapping in appreciation.

It was a visualization trick Granddad had taught him when he was a young pitcher about to face a particularly tough batter, and it had always worked. That reminded him to check that the tripod and video camera were still centered behind the rows of chairs. Since his grandparents weren't able to attend the show, he'd promised to record it and watch the video with them later. While it was a good solution, it only highlighted how frail his grandfather's health was, and that each day they had with him was precious.

Because it just might be the last.

Pushing those negative thoughts aside, Jason focused on Amy. She'd finished her rounds and caught his eye with an elegant nod. Giving her a thumbs-up, he went into the wings and dimmed the houselights, then brought them back up the way she'd requested. Folding his hands to keep them from shaking, he stood ready while she made her way onto the stage and waited for folks to find their seats and quiet down.

Extending her arms in a graceful dancer's pose, she said, "Welcome, everyone, to Arabesque. For those of you who don't know me, I'm Amy Morgan. My mother, Connie, and my aunt Helen—" she smiled at the beaming women seated front and center with Fred "—nourished my love of dance from the time I was a child. I'm honored to have had the opportunity to do the same with the group of very talented children you'll be seeing today."

A ripple of giggles passed behind the curtain, and

Jason smothered a grin as he stepped in and made the cut sign across his throat. Kids. What could you do?

"And so, it's with great pride that the Arabesque dance company presents to you our version of Tchaikovsky's beloved holiday ballet, *The Nutcracker.*"

That was his first cue, and Jason pulled the ropes that lifted the velvet drapes to bracket the dimly lit stage. After counting three Mississippis, he gradually increased the ballroom lights with one hand and brightened the tree decorations with the other. Somehow, he managed to accomplish that at the same rate so they all came up together the way they were supposed to.

Glancing across to the other wing area, he got a brilliant smile and the okay sign from Amy. Apparently, the producer was a little edgy, too, he mused. It was nice to know he wasn't the only one.

Since there were no adults in the production, willowy Heidi Peterson took her brightly colored wooden nutcracker from under the tree, floating around the stage with a delighted look on her face. As she went, she tossed in some exuberant jumps that reminded Jason of the pictures of Amy in her younger days. Judging by the nostalgic smile on her face, she was thinking the same thing.

Someday, he hoped to see that kind of joy in her again.

That thought caught him completely by surprise, and he did his best to shake it off and concentrate. Once Amy left for New York, the chances of him seeing her again were remote, at best. She'd be there for a while, rehabbing and then doing whatever it took to rejoin the world she'd so unwillingly left behind.

And he'd be in Barrett's Mill, a million miles from

the glitz and glamour she seemed to thrive on. He'd come to the conclusion that they wanted completely different things, and even if he could figure out what she needed to be truly happy, he had no clue how to make it happen.

The best he could do was hit all his marks today and do his part to make the show a success. After that, they'd celebrate the holiday with their families, and too soon it would be time to say goodbye. He'd been through many farewells in his life, and normally he accepted them as being for the best.

But this one would be different. Because hard as he'd tried not to let it happen, when Amy left, she'd be taking a piece of his heart with her.

The kids were doing a fabulous job. The trouble was, it was only intermission, and there were plenty of things that could still go wrong. First on the list: Brad's solo dance. He attacked it with the aggressiveness of an eight-year-old boy, and his delivery was still more pirate than prince, but Amy had finally decided to let him do it his own way. After all, the audience was made up of friends and family members. They'd love it no matter what he did.

While the show would be a nice end to the studio's fiscal year, to Amy the most important thing was for her students to get a taste of classical dance and discover they enjoyed it. Hopefully enough to continue taking classes and someday expose their own children to what Amy had adored ever since she could remember. Glancing over at the framed pictures on the wall brought to mind the excitement of the lights and being onstage, the fun of exploring a different world for a little while.

Those were the elements she recalled most fondly from her own childhood as a performer.

Oddly enough, the photos that used to make her sad now filled her with pride. Was it because she believed the new surgery could bring her back to that place? Or—

"They're doing great," Jason said as he hurried out from backstage. "How're you holding up?"

Only Jason would think to ask how she was faring, when she technically wasn't even a part of the show. His unerring thoughtfulness had touched her so many times, she'd lost track of the number. "I'm fine, thanks to you. Have you ever worked in a theater before?"

"Nah, I just catch on fast."

His hazel eyes twinkled at her with a little boy's enthusiasm, and she couldn't help laughing. "Lumberjack, carpenter, stage manager. Is there anything you can't do?"

"Actually, there is. I never learned how to waltz."

She laughed again and patted his arm. "I think I can help you with that before I go."

"I'm good at scaling trees, but music and counting steps aren't really my thing." Moving closer, he murmured, "I might need more attention than most of your students."

That sounded promising, she mused with a smile. But they were surrounded by people who were listening in while trying to appear engaged in their own conversations. Not to mention Brenda was at the snack table, and she'd been keeping an eye on them since Jason appeared. "I'm sure we can work something out. After tonight, the studio will be closing for the holidays, and I'll have time for a private lesson."

"How 'bout two?"

Oh, he was hard to resist, this towering man with the gentle heart. Endearing and determined all at once, with seemingly no effort at all, he'd reached the part of her that had shut down after her accident. The part that still looked eagerly into the future and believed that anything was possible if she wanted it badly enough.

Staring up at this incredibly generous man who'd drawn her out of herself and back into the world, she felt the tug of a new dream. One that had stubbornly wrapped itself around him and refused to let go. In the past, she never could have imagined something being more important to her than dancing. But now, here he was, standing in front of her with undisguised hope shining in his eyes. And in a flash of understanding, it hit her.

Jason wanted her to stay. He couldn't say that in front of all these people, of course, but his silent message was unmistakable. Shaken by that realization, she blurted, "Intermission is almost over. We should round up the kids for the dream scene."

"You got it, boss."

Flashing her a confident grin, he trotted up the steps and disappeared backstage. His cavalier behavior puzzled her, but she didn't have time to dissect it right now. Heading to the opposite wing, she gathered her troupe of flowers and sugar-plum fairies together, tweaking their costumes and making sure everyone had their slippers on the right feet.

When she met up with Brad, she stood in front of him and smiled. "You look awesome."

In his jaunty costume, with its plumed hat and rows of shiny gold buttons, he was a hybrid of toy soldier and swashbuckler. She congratulated herself on allowing him to wear his own black boots rather than dance shoes. After getting a fresh coat of polish, they topped off his outfit with jaunty style.

"Now, remember," she whispered while they waited for his entrance. "Clara's made of glass. Spin her gently."

"Okay," he squeaked, clearly anxious about his big solo.

Whenever someone told her not to be nervous, it only intensified her fear, so Amy gave his shoulders an encouraging shake. "Go on out there and show them what you've got."

Nodding, he entered the scene, tentatively at first, but growing more confident with each stride. By the time he reached the spotlight for his dance, his motions were fluid and right on the mark. She mentally took each step with him, willing him to remember them all. When he finished with a triumphant flourish, it looked more like a touchdown sign than ballet, but she couldn't possibly have cared less.

The audience broke into thunderous applause, and she motioned for the rest of the cast to hold their positions while Brad took a couple of impromptu bows. This was what it was all about, she thought as she traded thumbs-ups with Jason across the stage. As much as she loved performing, there was a unique satisfaction in teaching others those skills and watching them fly.

From that point on, the show flowed through the rest of Clara's dream, ending when she woke up back in the ballroom, asleep under the Christmas tree, clutching her beloved nutcracker. The curtains were still closing when the audience jumped to their feet, cheering and clapping, more than a few loudly whistling their appreciation.

Amy quickly assembled the cast behind the curtain, so overcome with joy, she had to steady her voice before speaking. "You guys are amazing," she praised them with a huge smile. "Now it's curtain-call time, but forget about what we practiced. Just go out there and have fun."

They all cheered at her suggestion, and she motioned for Jason to pull the curtains. To her surprise, though, the kids didn't run forward to ham it up in front of their adoring fans. Instead, they surrounded her in a group hug, moving her forward with them. Caught off guard, she had no choice but to follow along, fighting back a flood of tears that threatened to spill over.

She'd thought the crowd had been raucous enough before, but apparently they'd been holding back. People stood on their chairs, whooping and whistling, cheering for her along with the children. In all her years of performing, she'd never experienced anything like it. She chanced a look into the wings and saw Jason wearing a huge grin, clapping for all he was worth. When she motioned for him to come out, he shook his head and stayed put.

Despite all the work he'd done to make the show a success, he was refusing to share in the credit. He understood how much it meant to her, and he was willingly staying in the shadows to give her this moment in the spotlight. Jason was the first man she'd ever met who was secure enough to step back and allow someone else to shine.

Something told her it would be a long time before she met another one.

* * *

"Well, that about does it," Jason announced when he returned from packing up his truck. "All I have to do is hide that arbor from Gram for a few more days."

"What do you think she'll say when she finds out her Christmas present has been in full view of everyone in town all this time?" Amy asked.

"She'll laugh and tell me how clever I am, of course."

"Of course," Amy echoed, taking stock of their dismantling project. Without its holiday finery, Arabesque's facade had regained its classy, understated appearance. The effect should have pleased her, but for some reason it made her sad.

Jason must have noticed her expression, because he strolled over to stand beside her. "It looks nice."

"I guess," she allowed with a sigh. "I miss my nutcracker, though."

"You could take him to New York with you, like a souvenir."

Frowning, Amy shook her head. "Mom's apartment is pretty tiny, and I'll be staying with her for a while. He really belongs here, anyway."

The words rattled around in her head after she'd spoken them, making her wonder if the same sentiment applied to her. As the days passed and she faced the reality of leaving Barrett's Mill—and Jason—the temptation to stay grew stronger. Was it fear of the unknown? she wondered. Or was it something deeper than that?

"Hey, I've got an idea," Jason said, breaking the silence. When she looked at him, he grinned. "You don't have any more classes to teach, right?"

"No, we're done until after New Year's."

"Maybe now's a good time for that waltzing lesson we talked about."

Clearly, he was trying to distract her, to make her feel better about her questionable future. While she would have loved to spend some more time with him, she hesitated to torture them both with it. "Are you sure? I mean, you must have things to do out at the mill."

"Nothing that can't wait. Even my slave driver of a brother is letting up a little, now that all the holiday orders have gone out. Today, he and Chelsea are finishing up their Christmas shopping."

"Two days before?" Amy asked. "Are they crazy?"

"Tell me about it," he agreed with a laugh. "I wouldn't go near a mall right now."

The lighthearted exchange eased some of her concern, and she smiled. "Then it sounds like the ideal time for a dance lesson. As long as you have some other shoes to wear," she added with a glance down at the battered work boots on his feet.

"My church shoes are in my truck."

Church shoes, she thought with a little grin. He was so adorable sometimes. Then she caught on and narrowed her eyes with suspicion. "You planned on doing this now, didn't you?"

"Um…yeah."

He gave her a shameless grin, and she had to laugh. "Why on earth would you go to so much trouble? You've done so much for me, all you had to do was ask me for a lesson and I'd have gone along."

The grin widened, joined by the twinkling eyes that had captivated her more times than she could count. "It's more fun this way."

There was no point arguing with that, and she shook

her head. "Okay, go get your shoes. I'll meet you inside."

By the time he joined her, she'd cued up several waltz tracks on the stereo system. She'd already changed into dance shoes, so she took the opportunity to watch him do the same. For someone his size, he moved with an easy grace that had always impressed her. She'd seen those hands swing a hammer and tie a child's sneakers with equal skill, bringing a large measure of care to whatever task he chose.

He was such a remarkable man, she thought wistfully. Was she making a huge mistake walking away from him for some vague chance at normalcy?

When he stood to face her, his eager expression dimmed considerably. "What's wrong?"

"Nothing," she hedged, forcing optimism into her voice. "Just thinking about the traffic in New York."

"Busy, huh?" When she nodded, he said, "I'm sure you'll get used to it again in no time."

It was the perfect thing for him to say, of course, upbeat and positive. That was his nature, she'd come to realize, the way God had wired him so he could have a good life despite his rocky start. For the first time, she envied someone else's temperament, because being more easygoing would make things so much easier for her.

But maybe that wasn't the point, she mused while she fiddled with the music. Maybe God was giving her what she needed, too, but she was missing the big picture. Hopefully, when she was back in the environment she was more accustomed to, it would all make sense.

For now, she had a lesson to give, and she turned to

her eager student with a reassuring smile. "This won't hurt a bit."

"Not me, anyway," he commented with a chuckle. "I'll do my best not to squash those pretty little feet of yours."

When the music came on the speakers, he said, "Hey, I know this. It's from my niece's favorite Disney movie."

"*Sleeping Beauty* is another ballet by Tchaikovsky," she told him. "It's one of my favorites, too."

"Nice. Okay, what's first?"

She instructed him on how to stand, guiding his arm around her back while she put her hand in his. It looked like a child's hand nestled there, and the gentle way he held it made her heart sigh in contentment. Gazing up at him, she saw the same emotion playing over his face, lighting his eyes with the look she'd come to adore.

This was dangerous territory for two friends gamely trying to avoid getting entangled in something deeper that would end in a few days. The trouble was, being this close to him had fogged her mind so thoroughly, she was having a hard time remembering how the very simple dance began.

Once they got started, her training took over and she talked him through the rhythmic progression until he'd grasped it well enough to lead. "Don't count. Let the music flow through you and move your feet for you."

"Is that how it feels when you dance?" he asked with a curious look. When she nodded, he said, "I never really understood until just now. What's it like to just let go and follow where the music goes?"

"Amazing," she responded without even thinking. "It feels like you're part of something beautiful that takes you in and makes you special, too."

"Now I see why you miss it so much, why you want to get back to what you love. For you, it's like going home."

Astounded by his insight, she confided, "I'm happiest when I'm onstage. I always have been."

"It's where you belong. I noticed that during the show, when you were in the spotlight with the kids. You looked right out there."

"Is that why you stopped asking me to stay?" She'd resisted bringing up a sore subject, but since they were being so truthful with each other, it seemed like a good time.

"Yeah," he admitted with a heavy sigh. "That night after everything was over, it hit me that if I managed to convince you to forget about the surgery, you'd always wonder how your life would've been if you'd gone ahead with it. Sooner or later, you would've resented me for standing in your way and you'd hate me."

"I could never, ever hate you." Shaking his arms, she made sure she had his full attention before going on. "You weren't trying to stop me out of selfishness, but out of concern for me. I know that, and I appreciate it more than I can ever say."

"Yeah, I'm a real prince," he muttered.

"To me, you are." Part of her longed to ease his frown with a kiss, but she didn't want to muddy the friendship waters with such an intimate gesture. Instead, she reset her frame and smiled. "Would you like to try it one more time?"

He didn't respond at first, standing in front of her with his hands at his sides while he thought it over. She was keenly aware of how he must feel, wanting more time with her even though he knew it would only hurt more later when they had to say goodbye to each other. She felt the same way, and it was all she could do to put on a brave face while she waited for him to figure out what he wanted to do.

"Sure," he finally agreed, stepping into the position she'd shown him. "It's not every day a guy like me gets a private dance lesson with such a pretty teacher."

"Flattery will get you everywhere, Mr. Barrett," she simpered, batting her eyelashes for effect. "But my hourly rate is still the same."

Grinning, he retorted, "Seeing as I'm not paying you, does that mean I'm getting my money's worth?"

"I guess that's for you to decide."

The tense moment had passed, and she was relieved that their usual camaraderie had kicked back in. Although she enjoyed the next hour with him very much, the entire time a voice in the back of her mind was whispering to her:

Can you really leave all this behind?

Chapter Eleven

"I'm not sure about this," Rachel fretted when she and Jason arrived at the Crossroads Church on Christmas Eve. Standing in the entryway, she peered anxiously into the sanctuary dressed in its holiday finery and filled with people. "I mean, look at me."

She held out her arms, and Jason obliged by giving her a quick once-over. Since she'd been able to get more rest and eat properly, she looked much healthier than when she'd first arrived in town. *Plumper* was the description that came into his mind, but he figured that was the last thing a lady who was eight months pregnant wanted to hear. "I think you look nice. Is that dress new?"

Judging by her quick grin, she'd picked up on the fact that he'd sidestepped the obvious source of her concern. "When she was in town the other day, your sister-in-law Anne brought me a couple bags of maternity clothes. It was really generous of her to do that, considering."

"No one in my family considers all that except you. You're here now, and you've got a little person on the way. That's what matters to those folks in there," he chided her with a nod toward the open doors.

"I guess I'll have to take your word on that one."

"I've never lied to you, and I never will."

After a few more seconds, she let out a deep breath. "Okay. I'm ready."

"No one's perfect, Rachel," he reminded her gently. "What we do after our mistakes is what's most important."

"You're such a good guy," she said as they walked inside together. "I hope Amy knows that."

She did, but it wasn't enough. He was a straightforward country boy, and apparently he didn't have what it took to compete with her lifelong love of dancing. Hopefully, before too long he'd come to terms with that and be able to think of her fondly. Right now, though, knowing he didn't measure up made him wish he had more to offer her. Since he didn't, he was going to have to swallow his objections and let her go.

He escorted Rachel to the section where his family was sitting in a group across two pews. Like the gentleman he'd raised them all to be, Dad stood and moved into the aisle. "Would you like to join us, Rachel? We've got a seat right here for you."

Eyes wide with gratitude, she nodded in reply and slid in next to Jason's mother. Putting an arm around their guest the way she did with everyone she met, Mom said, "Merry Christmas Eve, honey. How are you and the baby doing these days?"

"Dr. Peterson says we're both fine," Rachel answered politely. "Thank you for asking."

"We always have a gathering back at the house after

church," Mom continued. "If you're not too tired, we'd love to have you come by for a while."

Rachel cast a hesitant look at Jason, and he said, "No one should be alone at Christmas, Rachel. It's up to you, though."

Clearly overwhelmed by the gesture, she looked from one of his parents to the other with a faint smile. "That sounds wonderful. Thank you again."

Satisfied, Jason left Rachel chatting with his family, trusting them to make sure she wouldn't feel like an outsider in the congregation full of strangers. Then he yanked his nicely knotted tie off to the side and trotted up the risers. Moving carefully through the rapidly filling row, he landed at the opposite end of the tenor section from where he normally stood. That put him next to the sopranos. And Amy.

She gave him a curious look, and he grinned back. "Hey there."

"Hey yourself." The beautiful smile she gave him drove the last of his sadness away, at least for now. "Did you come over here for a reason?"

"To tell you how incredible you look in that dress. Green's my favorite color, y'know." She didn't respond, and he shook his head with a chuckle. "Let me guess. Chelsea filled you in."

"Maybe, but I bought the dress. Was that all you needed?"

His strategy for getting a few moments with her had slipped his mind, but he quickly recovered. "Mom's busy, and my tie's gone all wonky. Think you can help me out?"

"You mean, the tie you yanked out of place on your

way up here?" she teased as she went up a step so she could reach to pull it loose and start over.

"Busted," he admitted with a laugh, pleased to hear her join in.

She quickly got serious, though. "I see Rachel's here."

Here we go again, he thought with a sigh. "I know you won't be crazy about this, but I invited her to come tonight, and Mom asked her over to the house afterward. She's got no one else to spend Christmas with."

"So she's celebrating it with you," Amy sniped in a tone that made it clear she liked the idea even less than he'd anticipated.

"Not really."

"How do you figure that?"

"I'm spending mine with you," he told her with a smile. "Rachel's just gonna be one of the hundred or so guests at my grandparents' party tonight."

After taking a moment to absorb that, her expression softened and she continued in a less combative tone, "It was nice of you to seat her with your family. I mean, if anyone can understand what she's going through, it'll be your mom."

Considering how she felt about Rachel, Amy's generosity amazed him. "I thought so, too. But I'm glad you get it."

"Oh, I do," she assured him with a quick laugh. "I'm still not wild about the whole thing, but I get it."

In his mind, he heard Fred Morgan grousing about the women in his family being able to drive a man straight over the edge. Now that Jason had firsthand knowledge of it, he marveled at how the mechanic had remained his easygoing self all these years. With a grin, he said, "Guess I'll just have to take what I can get."

"Hold it right there," Brenda ordered, lining up a shot with her camera phone. Checking the result, she sighed. "You two are just too adorable."

Ignoring her cousin, Amy finished shoring up his tie and tapped his nose with her finger. "All set."

"Thanks." They'd never been level with each other this way, and judging by the smirk on her face, she found it as amusing as he did. "You like being as tall as me, don't you?"

Glancing around the church, she said, "It's quite the view from up here, isn't it?"

"Yeah, it is."

Those incredible eyes came back to him, glimmering with something he'd never seen in them until tonight. Not tears, he realized, but emotion. A mixture of joy and sorrow, the same as he was feeling. Fortunately, the pastor walked through the door behind the altar into the chapel, and Mrs. Griggs motioned for the choir to take their places.

Jason offered Amy a hand down, keeping her hand in his until she was standing beside him again. And then, reluctantly, he released her. The wistful look she gave him must have mirrored his own, and he dredged up a grin, hoping to make her feel better. She responded with a flicker of her usual smile, and then it was time for them to sing.

Normally, the Christmas Eve service was his favorite one of the entire year. Filled with warmth and hope for a better future, it encompassed all the things his family had taught him to value. But this time, even Pastor

Griggs's touching sermon on God's never-ending love for His children wasn't enough to lift Jason's spirits.

All he could think of was Amy leaving. And how empty his life was going to feel without her in it.

Following the service, Amy and Jason began a leisurely stroll toward his grandparents' house. Diane had flown from the church with Rachel and everyone else in tow, hurrying back to make certain everything would be ready for the Christmas Eve party that was apparently an annual Barrett tradition.

"I wish they would've let me help," Amy ventured to break the silence.

"Someone must've told them you can't cook."

The sarcastic edge on his voice clued her in that he'd been the one to warn them off, but she really couldn't blame him. He didn't want her poisoning his family during the holidays. Totally understandable. "I could carry dishes in to stock the buffet or wrangle kids or something."

Smiling down at her, he took her hand gently in his much larger one. "You're coming as my guest. Guests are supposed to relax and enjoy themselves."

Returning that smile came so naturally to her now, she could barely recall feeling self-conscious around him. But she had, and he'd patiently drawn her out, encouraging her, cheering her on, until she'd learned to trust him without question. When they reached the square, she paused to admire the town's tree one last time.

"Do you remember the Starlight Festival?" she asked.

Chuckling, he wrapped an arm loosely around her

shoulders. "Sure. It was the best one ever 'cause you were there."

Blushing at the compliment, she nearly swallowed what she wanted to say next. But she forged ahead because there was something very important she wanted him to know. Turning, she met his eyes, saw the honest affection he felt for her twinkling warmly in them.

"That night, I told you things I haven't shared with anyone, not even my mother. You didn't even blink, just accepted everything about me the way it was. Your attitude made me believe other people could do the same, and I'll always be grateful to you for doing that."

"Since we're here—" he reached into the pocket of his suit jacket "—I have something for you. I was planning to give it to you later, but this seems like the right place for it."

Amy took the small box wrapped in shiny gold paper, then fished in her purse for the one she'd brought for him. They looked similar, and he laughed. "I hope they're not the same thing."

"Me, too."

They tore their gifts open at the same time, and Amy opened her box with a little creak. Inside, on a cushion of burgundy velvet, she found a pair of crystal earrings fashioned into multifaceted stars. They looked remarkably like the sterling-silver tie tack she'd gotten for him, and she couldn't help laughing. "We seem to have similar taste in jewelry."

"Does that mean you like 'em?" In answer, she reached up and drew his face to hers for a grateful kiss. She felt his lips quirk into one of those grins, and he murmured, "I really like the way you say thank-you."

Gathering her into his arms, he gave her a longer,

deeper kiss. Savoring the warmth of being surrounded by him, she had a hunch the effect of those stolen kisses would linger far past Christmas Eve. Footsteps approached them, and she knew without looking who'd stopped to say hello.

"Nice tree, isn't it?" Uncle Fred asked in a casual tone that did little to mask his true purpose for pausing here at that exact moment.

Eyes still locked on her, Jason replied, "Very nice."

"So we'll see you at the Barretts' party, then," Aunt Helen chimed in.

"Oh, leave them be," Mom scolded, shooing them away. To Amy, she whispered, "It's a beautiful night for stargazing. You two just take your time."

She continued on with her brother and sister-in-law in tow, and Jason commented, "I guess they've got us pegged."

"I'm so glad we got some time together before I have to go." Resting her hand on his jaw, she frowned as the impact of her choice hit her full force. "I'm really going to miss you."

"You could stay," he suggested in a voice tinged with hope. He hadn't done that recently, and the temptation to say yes was so strong, she didn't trust herself to speak. When she didn't respond, he sighed. "But that would mean you'd have to give up on ever dancing again."

"I pray someday you'll understand why I'm doing this."

"I already do," he muttered as he stepped away from her. "That's what makes it so hard for me. I want you here, but I want you to be happy even more. If that means you have to go somewhere else, I'll just have to learn to live with it."

He took her hand again, and they walked the rest of the way in silence. Blinking back tears, Amy wished she was one of those people who could be satisfied with second best. She'd always considered her unrelenting drive to be an asset. Accompanied by years of hard work, it had propelled her to heights most people could only imagine, and she was tremendously proud of what she'd accomplished as a performer.

But tonight, seeing how much her ambition was hurting someone she cared about, she was beginning to have her doubts.

Even before they reached Will and Olivia's house, she could see it was lit up like one of Macy's famous holiday window displays. Cars lined both sides of the street, and the sounds of laughing conversation mixed with Christmas music floated out on the night air.

People were standing on the front porch with food and drinks, and through the open front door she saw dozens more in the dining room. "Half the town must be here!"

"It's Christmas Eve," he said, as if that explained everything.

"Are you sure this isn't too much for your grandparents?"

"It's just what they need," he assured her as they went up the front steps. "Too much quiet drives 'em bonkers, and besides, we always do the party here. After the kids open their gifts at home in the morning, everyone comes back here for lunch and presents."

Since moving away, she and Mom had quietly celebrated the holidays together, so Amy wasn't used to large family gatherings like this one. What Jason described struck her as something out of a classic Christmas movie, and she smiled. "It sounds perfect."

"Not really. Something goes wrong at one point or another, but we have a lotta fun."

Bulldozing ahead of her, he made a path for her to follow to a buffet table loaded down with roast beef, all manner of veggies, three varieties of homemade rolls and three of the biggest hams she'd ever seen. It took a while for them to get through the line, but every morsel smelled as if it would be totally worth the wait. Once they had their food, Jason angled his way into the living room, where they found Will and Olivia in the place of honor near the tree.

"Here they are," Olivia announced, as if they'd been waiting all night just to see the two of them. "I told you they'd be along soon."

"I hope you took this lovely girl for a stroll," Will said with a wink at his youngest grandson.

"Yes, sir. Just like you taught me."

While they chatted back and forth, the fondness that rippled between Jason and the grandparents who'd taken him into their hearts was touching to see. Raised with so much love around him, it took very little effort to picture him with a family of his own someday. Enjoying the holidays, honoring the faith that was such an important part of who he was.

The woman he chose to share that life with him would be blessed beyond measure. Surrounded by the warmth of the Barrett family's traditional Christmas, Amy only wished there was some way that woman could be her.

"I look like death warmed over," Amy complained as she scowled into the hallway mirror in her mother's chic Manhattan apartment. "When I go to the hospital for my physical tomorrow, they're going to think I'm sick or something."

Mom, who was whipping up some dinner for them, stepped out of her galley kitchen for a look. When she frowned, Amy knew her concerns were on the mark. "I hate to say this, sweetie, but you look like you haven't slept since we left Barrett's Mill."

She hadn't, at least not very well. She spent most of her nights tossing and turning, her mind going over and over all the things that could go wrong with her surgery. As if that wasn't enough, when she tried to conjure up something more pleasant so she could rest, the space behind her eyes filled with Jason's face.

Jason grinning at her, laughing with her at something one of the kids had done, gazing down at her with that adoring look she'd give anything to see one more time. She'd expected that longing to gradually fade, but instead it was getting stronger. She missed his strong presence and the comforting knack he had for showing up just when she needed him.

Quite honestly, she was having second thoughts about her decision to reclaim some of her past. Because that part of her life had nothing to do with him, as the days dragged by she was beginning to think that might not be what she wanted anymore.

Wiping her hands on a towel, Mom settled on one of the stools at the stylish breakfast bar that separated her kitchen from the small living area overlooking the city. Amy had always loved that view, but over the past few months she'd grown accustomed to trees and sprawling, old-fashioned houses, with plenty of open space to roam around in.

"Come talk to me," her mother nudged, patting the other stool. "Tell me what's wrong."

"Everything." Suddenly, she felt as if she was ten again, trudging home from a rough day at school or rehearsal. Climbing onto the stool, she fought the impulse to drop her head onto the counter and weep. "Mostly, I'm confused."

"About?"

"Everything," Amy repeated ruefully. Realizing she wasn't being very helpful, she searched for words to explain how she was feeling. "I'm not sure what I want anymore."

"Because of Jason?" When Amy nodded, Mom gave her a wise smile. "He's a wonderful young man. I wasn't in town that long, but I could see how much he cares for you. Do you feel the same way about him?"

Amy nodded, tears welling in her eyes. "At first, he was completely against me trying this procedure because it's so risky. But after a while, he realized how important it was to me and said he just wanted me to be happy."

"What a generous thing to do. It's not everyone who can put their own feelings aside and do what's best for someone else."

"I know," Amy responded, more miserable than ever. "What do you think I should do?"

Standing, Mom went over the coatrack and grabbed their jackets. "I think we should take a walk. Let's get some lattes and go to Rockefeller Center."

"I don't think—"

"Don't argue with your mother," she scolded with a wink. "Just put your coat on and let's go."

By the time they'd stopped for coffees and made

their way to the holiday hub of New York, the knots in Amy's thoughts had begun to loosen up a bit. They strolled along, admiring the decorations and watching the skaters on the ice rink below. They chatted about the after-Christmas sales and whether the forecast for a dusting of snow would prove accurate or not. Basically, they discussed any topic that had absolutely nothing to do with Amy's dilemma, and she welcomed the distraction.

When they reached the walkway near the famous tree, they paused for a few moments. This time last year, Amy had been deep into her rehab and couldn't make the trek here, so it had been a while since she'd last seen it. The tree itself was enormous, strung with thousands of lights and topped with a custom-made star spun from the finest crystal in the world.

But to her surprise, it had lost some of the appeal it once held for her. Instead, she was recalling a more modest version, tucked into a square in a Blue Ridge town so small, most outsiders had no idea it even existed. Her memory flashed to Christmas Eve with Jason, and she fingered one of the earrings he'd given her. Thinking back over their time together, she found herself wishing she could rewind to that heartwarming evening and make it last just a little longer. And that was when she knew.

She was in love with Jason Barrett.

Despite the fact that they had almost nothing in common, somehow they'd forged a bond that still connected them across hundreds of miles. She longed to hear his mellow drawl, see the twinkle in his eyes when he looked at her. Mostly, she wanted to be circled in his arms, the place where she felt treasured and safe.

"I'm going back," she blurted, hesitantly eyeing her mother to gauge her reaction. When she got a knowing smile, she let out a relieved breath. "You knew that, didn't you?"

"I was hoping you'd come to that. What changed your mind?"

"My heart," she answered simply. "I love Jason, and I want to be with him."

"Life doesn't always go the way we want it to. What will you do if things don't work out between you two?"

"They will. I'll make sure of it."

"That's my girl." Laughing, Mom hugged her around her shoulders. "Let's go make some reservations."

Amy stared at her in disbelief. "Does that mean you're coming with me?"

"Are you kidding? I wouldn't miss this for the world."

"Jason," Chelsea said from the open doorway that led to the front of the mill house. "It's New Year's Eve. What are you doing here?"

Keeping his eyes on the gears he was oiling, he asked, "What are *you* doing here? Shouldn't you and Paul be doing the dressing-up thing for Mom's shindig tonight?"

"Olivia sent me to find you." Coming into the production area, she sat down on a nearby stool and waited for him to look up at her. "She's worried about you, and frankly, so am I. You haven't been yourself since Amy left."

The sound of her name set off a twisting sensation in his chest, and he winced. "I thought I'd skip this one. I'm not really in a celebrating mood."

"I sympathize with you, but this party is important to the family. You know that."

That knot tightened even more, and he swallowed hard around the lump in his throat. He'd never known his birth parents, and his adoptive grandfather was dying. Add to that the sense of loss he felt over Amy, and it was almost more than he could bear. Even his natural optimism wasn't enough to overcome the clouds hanging over him these days.

Looking over at Chelsea, seeing the compassion in her eyes, he relented with a sigh. "Okay, I'll be there."

She gave him an encouraging smile, then stood and folded her hands, waiting. When he realized what she was up to, he had to chuckle. "You're gonna follow me into town, aren't you?"

"Yes, I am."

"Does that work with my big brother when you want him to do something?" Jason asked as he flipped off lights on their way out the front door.

She gave him a proud, feminine smile. "Yes, it does. But don't tell him I said so. He likes thinking all those things are his idea."

They both laughed, and Jason was in a slightly better frame of mind by the time they reached his grandparents' house. They went in through the kitchen, and after greeting his mom, he took the back stairs three at a time to go up to his room and change into something more presentable for company.

Dressed and ready for the evening ahead, he took the front stairs and pulled up short halfway down.

"Amy?"

Like a vision straight out of his dreams, she balanced a dainty hand on the old newel post and bathed him in the most incredible smile he'd ever seen. She didn't say anything, but the emotions shining in her eyes were enough to make him nearly trip over his own feet as he hurried down the rest of the steps.

Although he knew people were watching them, he took her in his arms for a long, grateful hug. Holding her away, he looked her over to make sure he was really awake. "What are you doing here?"

"It's New Year's Eve," she replied, as if that should've been obvious to him. She placed a hand on his cheek, and this smile had a melancholy quality to it. "I missed you."

No one outside his family had ever gone to so much trouble to do something for him, and it touched him in a way he'd never expected. It was far from midnight, but he didn't care. Reeling her back in, he gave her a long-overdue kiss. Resting his forehead on hers, he murmured, "I missed you, too."

"Why didn't you call and tell me?"

"I didn't want you to think I was going back on my word, trying to convince you to live here and run the studio."

Tilting her head with a curious expression, she asked, "And now?"

"I love you," he answered instinctively, not stopping to consider how crazy it would sound to her. "I know it hasn't been that long, and you probably want to get to know me better—"

She interrupted him with a finger over his lips. "You, Jason Barrett, are the sweetest, kindest man I've ever met. I think I fell in love with you that first day, when you stepped in to rescue my show and fix all the things that were wrong in my apartment. It just took me a while to realize it."

Jason was so stunned by her revelation, he hardly dared to believe it. "You mean, all those arguments we had were for nothing?"

"They were fun," she corrected him with a playful grin. "Most folks back down when I get stubborn, but you roll up your sleeves and keep on fighting. I like that about you."

"Go figure."

It sounded to him as if she'd made some kind of decision, that this was more than a quick visit for a kiss at midnight. Trying to curb his excitement, he asked, "When do you head back for your surgery?"

"I gave it a lot of thought while I was gone," she confided. "But dancing isn't the right thing for me anymore. Being here is what I want."

Something more was sparkling in her eyes, and he took a shot. "With me?"

"With you."

As they stood there smiling at each other, a flash went off, and he saw Amy's mom checking the screen on her camera phone. Beaming, she gave them a quick wave and sauntered into the kitchen. Judging by his mother's delighted reaction, she liked the result, too.

"You'll have to excuse her," Amy said with a sigh. "Her picture's next to the definition of *hopeless romantic* in the dictionary."

They both laughed, and it occurred to him that he was the only one there who was surprised to see her. Now Gram sending someone to fetch him from the mill made total sense. "Gram knew you were here, didn't she?"

"Yes. I wanted to make sure she and Will were okay with me crashing the party."

"So you just assumed I'd be cool with it?"

In reply, she gave him that cute little smirk of hers, and he shook his head in defeat. Sliding an arm around her shoulders, he proudly escorted her into the living room, where the party was getting started. As midnight approached, Gram turned on the TV and they all gathered around for the big countdown.

"Don't you miss being there in person?" he asked Amy, nodding at the insane crowd gathered in Times Square.

"You're kidding, right? I wouldn't go anywhere near Times Square tonight. If I went into that mess, someone would squish me like a bug. Mom and I always watch it on TV, too."

"How 'bout that? Guess you learn something every day."

Standing behind Amy with his arms wrapped around the woman he loved more than anything, Jason had never been happier in his life. When the ball finally reached the bottom of its pole and burst into an array of sparkling lights, Amy spun around for a long kiss filled with unspoken promises for their future together.

Best New Year's ever.

Epilogue

"I told you I make a fabulous matron of honor," Brenda gloated, handing Amy the bouquet she was going to toss for the single women clustered in Will and Olivia's large dining room.

"Yes, you did. With all the practice you've had, you should go pro."

"What a spectacular job that would be." Her romantic cousin sighed.

Laughing, Amy spun around and heaved the flowers backward. Then she glanced over her shoulder to see who got them. Jenna looked as stunned to find them in her hands as the other girls did when they realized they'd missed.

Waving them over her head, she called out, "Who wants 'em?"

A dozen squealing women clamored for another chance, and she covered her eyes before throwing the bouquet into the fray. Turning away before they were caught, she grinned over at Amy and wiped pretend sweat from her forehead.

"You make it sound like getting married is some kind of torture," Amy chided her as Jason joined them.

"For you, no. Me, absolutely," her friend replied with a shudder.

"Jenna's a free spirit," Jason agreed. "I feel sorry for any guy who thinks he can't live without her."

"By the way, you two," she needled with her usual sarcasm. "Getting married on Valentine's Day? How cliché is that?"

Amy laughed at the sour face she made. "I always thought it would be fun to have a Valentine's wedding. This way Jason will never forget our anniversary."

"Like you'd let me," he scoffed.

Pinning him with a flinty glare, Jenna warned, "Just make sure you remember what I said, JB. If you don't treat Amy right, we're gonna have a serious problem, you and me."

With that, she sailed toward the buffet and started messing with Paul.

Jason let out a relieved whistle. "I'm not too proud to admit that woman scares me."

"She scares everyone," Amy assured him, fluffing the baby's breath on his boutonniere. Seeing it reminded her to ask, "How are Rachel and her little girl doing?"

"Doc said they're fit as a couple of fiddles. Those extra couple weeks almost drove Rachel bonkers, but in the end, everything turned out fine. They might stop by later, if that's okay."

Just a few weeks ago, Amy would have bitten her tongue and gone along to please him. Now that she was his wife, she was feeling much more gracious. "Of course. I'd love to meet the baby. Eva, right?"

"Yeah. It's some kind of family name, I guess."

"Eva McCarron." Amy tested it out loud. "Very pretty. If she looks anything like her mother, that girl is going to be absolutely stunning when she grows up."

"You're being really great about Rachel deciding to stay here in town," he commented in a wary voice. "Is there a reason for that?"

In answer, she held out her left hand and wiggled her fingers so the gold rings he'd given her sparkled in the overhead lights.

"It all makes sense now," he replied with a grin. "In case you're interested, I was just talking to Joe Stegall from the hardware store, and he said those roofing joists I ordered came in this morning. With the mill cranking out everything else, we should be able to break ground on the addition behind Arabesque anytime now."

"When we were getting ready upstairs, Chelsea was telling me the orders for spring are finally ramping up. That means they're going to need more of your time soon," Amy argued. "The furniture business means a lot to the whole town, so the expansion can wait until your workload there dies down a little."

"Are you sure you want to put it off? You're used to living in that apartment by yourself, so it's probably gonna feel pretty cramped in there with the two of us."

Being anywhere by herself was the furthest thing from her mind these days, Amy thought with a smile. "We'll figure it out, the same way we've done with everything else. I don't want you taking on too much and not having any time for your wife," she added, snaking her arms around his waist for a squeeze.

"My wife," he echoed with a quick kiss. "I kinda like the sound of that."

"Me, too."

"Especially since that means we get to go on a honeymoon."

"Which is where?" she asked. When he grinned and shook his head, she grabbed his lapels for a thorough shake. "I know you're Mr. Spontaneous, but you can't spring something like that on me. I'm a girl, and I need to know what sort of clothes to bring."

"Just bring a little of everything."

"Are you trying to get us into our first married fight?" she demanded in mock anger. "Because if you don't quit yanking my chain, that's where we're headed, mister."

"Well, I'd hate for you to cause a scene in front of all these people. It's warm, with lots of water but no sand." She motioned for more, and he relented with a chuckle. "Okay, you win. You said you've never been on a cruise, so we're taking one of those big, fancy ships to the Bahamas. Only a few days, like we agreed, in case something happens and the family needs us here."

A constant for all the Barretts, the ongoing concern for Will had deepened since the holidays. Unable to sit upright on his own, he maintained his customarily positive attitude even while his condition was worsening. Amy didn't know how he managed it with the pain he must be in, but his acceptance of the inevitable boosted the spirits of those around him.

None of them knew when the end would come, but they could all see it advancing a little every day. Everyone had made a determined effort to celebrate Jason and Amy's engagement and wedding, but they'd missed out on some of the joy having a new couple in the circle should have brought them. Still, families stood together through good times and bad, rejoicing over some things and mourning others.

That was what made the Barretts so strong, Amy had come to understand. You weren't born with that kind of perspective. You acquired it by accepting what God handed you and doing the best you could with it.

Seeking to change the subject, she summoned a positive tone. "I have to tell you, it's very handy being married to a guy who knows how to build things. Without you, *The Nutcracker* might never have happened, and all those kids would've been so disappointed. That would've been such a shame, don't you think?"

Jason eyed her suspiciously. "I know that look. What've you got in mind?"

"Our Christmas show was such a roaring success, I was toying with the idea of doing another children's ballet in the spring. I thought back through the ones I danced in when I was younger, and a few of them could easily be scaled down to their level. Since so many of them already know the story of Sleeping Beauty and her prince, I think they'd really enjoy that one."

"Not to mention it's one of the director's favorites. What kind of scenery are we talking about?"

Reaching back into her memory, she began describing the forest scene and lavish castle where the heroic prince finds Sleeping Beauty in a tower, still under the witch's spell. "They won't want to do the kiss, of course, but I'll come up with another way for him to wake her up. We'll need a spinning wheel, and I'm sure Aunt Helen and I will be able to remake some of the sugar-plum costumes for the cast. To make the castle walls look like stone, we can use the same faux painting technique on them that you did on the fireplace for the *Nutcracker* ballroom, and—"

Laughing, Jason held up his hands in a T. "Time-out, sweetheart. We've been married for all of ten minutes, and I haven't had anything to eat since breakfast. Could we put off sketching out the set designs until after we have some food?"

"Sure," she told him with a light kiss. "Whenever you want."

He grinned down at her. "Are you seriously giving up control to let me pick when we start on this?"

"You sound surprised."

"Well—"

"Are you seriously trying to start a fight with me on our wedding day?" she teased, echoing his earlier question.

"Umm, no?"

Sliding her arms around him, she gave him a quick hug. "Good answer."

* * * * *

Dear Reader,

Thanks so much for stopping by Barrett's Mill for the holidays! Things can get pretty hectic at the end of the year, and I really appreciate you fitting this sweet story into your spare time.

While preparing to write a Christmas book, I sift through our family traditions for special memories. One of those is *The Nutcracker,* which has been a favorite of mine since childhood. The beautiful music, the costumes, the incredibly graceful dancers…they all sweep me into a magical place and time where anything is possible.

For Amy, who's lost her direction in more ways than one, each day is about trudging along a path she never would've chosen for herself. It takes Jason and his own unshakable faith to show her that even though her new life isn't what she'd planned, that doesn't mean it's bad. In fact, some of the things she's discovered along the way—namely, him—only came to her when she gave up on her dancing career. Drawing on his quiet strength, she's finally able to put her sparkling past behind her and embrace an even more meaningful future with him.

If you'd like to stop by for a visit, you'll find me online at www.miaross.com, Facebook, Twitter and Goodreads. While you're there, send me a message in your favorite format. I'd love to hear from you!

Merry Christmas,
Mia Ross

Questions for Discussion

1. At the beginning of the story, Amy's not thrilled with her new job but is trying to make the best of it. Have you ever been in a similar situation? How did you handle it?

2. Even though he enjoys logging, Jason returns to Barrett's Mill to help out with the family business. Do you think he's happy with that decision, or does he wish he could have stayed in Oregon?

3. Christmas is a special time for families, and this one is even more so for the Barretts because of Will's declining health. Has your own family been through a similar time? What did you do to make memories that would last?

4. Jason remembers seeing Amy in a dance production when they were very young. What is the earliest memory you have? Why do you think it's stayed with you through the years?

5. *The Nutcracker* is a special holiday tradition for Amy, and she does her best to make it memorable for the kids in her show. Which Christmas events do you enjoy year after year? Why?

6. When his grandmother falls and injures her arm, Jason feels guilty for not being there to help her.

Many of us have elderly relatives and have experience with this kind of situation. If you're one of those, how do you handle it?

7. Because she felt abandoned by God, Amy began to question her faith. With Jason's help, she comes to terms with her situation and comes back to the fold. Has someone you know ever experienced this? What did it take to change their mind?

8. Jason's adoption by the Barretts was an unusual but loving arrangement, and he's glad to be part of their family. Are you an adoptive or foster parent or grandparent? Why did you choose to take on this responsibility?

9. When Rachel shows up desperate for Jason's help, Amy has a hard time understanding why he'd help someone who treated him so badly in the past. Which stance would you take? Why?

10. The town of Barrett's Mill is a throwback to simpler times, which is one reason people enjoy living there. Of all the places you've lived, which is your favorite?

11. By the end of the story, Amy realizes she enjoys teaching dance much more than she'd expected to. If you could choose to be a performer or a teacher, which would you rather be?

12. Amy's always dreamed of being married on Valentine's Day, and Jason's happy to oblige her. Is there something like that on your own bucket list? If so, what is it?

COMING NEXT MONTH FROM
Love Inspired®

Available December 16, 2014

HER COWBOY HERO
Refuge Ranch • by Carolyne Aarsen

When rodeo cowboy Tanner Fortier ropes ex-fiancée Keira Bannister into fixing his riding saddle, the reunited couple just might have a chance to repair their lost love.

SMALL-TOWN FIREMAN
Gordon Falls • by Allie Pleiter

Karla Kennedy is eager to leave Gordon Falls, but working with hunky fireman Dylan MacDonald on the firehouse anniversary celebration has this city girl rethinking her small-town future.

SECOND CHANCE REUNION
Village of Hope • by Merrillee Whren

After a troubled past, Annie Payton is on the road to recovery. Now she must convince her ex-husband she's worthy of his forgiveness—and a second chance at love.

LAKESIDE REDEMPTION
by Lisa Jordan

Zoe James returns home to Shelby Lake for a fresh start—not romance. So when she starts to fall for ex-cop Caleb Sullivan, will she have the courage to accept a second chance at happily-ever-after?

HEART OF A SOLDIER
Belle Calhoune

Soldier Dylan Hart can't wait to surprise pen-pal Holly Lynch in her hometown. But when he discovers that sweet Holly has kept a big secret from him, can their budding romance survive?

THE RANCHER'S CITY GIRL
Patricia Johns

Cory Stone's determined to build a relationship with his estranged father, but when he invites the ill man to join him at his ranch, Cory never expects to find love with his dad's nurse.

LOOK FOR THESE AND OTHER LOVE INSPIRED BOOKS WHEREVER BOOKS ARE SOLD, INCLUDING MOST BOOKSTORES, SUPERMARKETS, DISCOUNT STORES AND DRUGSTORES.

LICNM1214

REQUEST YOUR FREE BOOKS!

2 FREE INSPIRATIONAL NOVELS
PLUS 2
FREE
MYSTERY GIFTS

Love Inspired

YES! Please send me 2 FREE Love Inspired® novels and my 2 FREE mystery gifts (gifts are worth about $10). After receiving them, if I don't wish to receive any more books, I can return the shipping statement marked "cancel." If I don't cancel, I will receive 6 brand-new novels every month and be billed just $4.74 per book in the U.S. or $5.24 per book in Canada. That's a saving of at least 21% off the cover price. It's quite a bargain! Shipping and handling is just 50¢ per book in the U.S. and 75¢ per book in Canada.* I understand that accepting the 2 free books and gifts places me under no obligation to buy anything. I can always return a shipment and cancel at any time. Even if I never buy another book, the two free books and gifts are mine to keep forever.

105/305 IDN F47Y

Name _____ (PLEASE PRINT) _____

Address _____ Apt. #

City _____ State/Prov. _____ Zip/Postal Code

Signature (if under 18, a parent or guardian must sign)

Mail to the Harlequin® Reader Service:
IN U.S.A.: P.O. Box 1867, Buffalo, NY 14240-1867
IN CANADA: P.O. Box 609, Fort Erie, Ontario L2A 5X3

**Are you a subscriber to Love Inspired books
and want to receive the larger-print edition?
Call 1-800-873-8635 or visit www.ReaderService.com.**

* Terms and prices subject to change without notice. Prices do not include applicable taxes. Sales tax applicable in N.Y. Canadian residents will be charged applicable taxes. Offer not valid in Quebec. This offer is limited to one order per household. Not valid for current subscribers to Love Inspired books. All orders subject to credit approval. Credit or debit balances in a customer's account(s) may be offset by any other outstanding balance owed by or to the customer. Please allow 4 to 6 weeks for delivery. Offer available while quantities last.

Your Privacy—The Harlequin® Reader Service is committed to protecting your privacy. Our Privacy Policy is available online at www.ReaderService.com or upon request from the Harlequin Reader Service.

We make a portion of our mailing list available to reputable third parties that offer products we believe may interest you. If you prefer that we not exchange your name with third parties, or if you wish to clarify or modify your communication preferences, please visit us at www.ReaderService.com/consumerchoice or write to us at Harlequin Reader Service Preference Service, P.O. Box 9062, Buffalo, NY 14269. Include your complete name and address.

LI13R

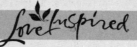
Keira wished she could keep her hands from trembling as she handled Tanner's saddle. What was wrong with her?

Seeing him again, his brown eyes edged with sooty lashes and framed by the slash of dark brows, the hard planes of his face emphasized by the stubble shadowing his jaw and cheeks, brought back painful memories Keira thought she had put aside.

He looked the same and yet different. Harder. Leaner. He wore his sandy brown hair longer; it brushed the collar of his shirt, giving him reckless look at odds with the Tanner she had once known.

And loved.

She sucked in a rapid breath as she turned over the saddle on the table. Tanner seemed to fill the cramped shop.

Keep your focus on your work, she reminded herself.

"So? What's the verdict?" Tanner asked.

"I don't know if it's worth fixing this," she said, quietly. "It'll be a lot of work."

Tanner sighed. "But can you fix it?"

"I'd need to take it apart to see. If that's the case, two weeks?".

"That's cutting it close," Tanner said. "Is it possible to get it done quicker?"

Keira would have preferred not to work on it at all. It would mean that Tanner would be around more often.

It had taken her years to relegate Tanner to the shadowy recesses of her mind. She didn't know if she could see him more often and maintain any semblance of the hard-won peace she now experienced. Tanner was too connected to memories she had spent hours in prayer trying to bury.

"I'm gonna need it for the National Finals in Vegas in a couple of weeks." Tanner continued.

"I heard you're still doing mechanic work, as well?" She was pleasantly surprised she could chitchat with Tanner, the man who had once held her heart.

"Yup, except last year I bought out the owner. Now I'm the boss, which means I can take off when I want. I took over the shop in Sheridan after a good rodeo run. The same one I started working on before—" He didn't need to finish. Keira knew exactly what "before" was.

Before that summer when she left Tanner and Saddlebank without allowing him the second chance he so desperately wanted. Before that summer when everything changed.

A heavy silence dropped between them as solid as a wall. Keira turned away, burying the memories deep, where they couldn't taunt her.

But Tanner's very presence teased them to the surface.

She looked up at him to tell him she couldn't work on the saddle, but as she did she felt a jolt of awareness as their eyes met. She tried to tear her gaze away, but it was as if the old bond that had once connected them still bound them to each other.

Will Keira agree to fix Tanner's saddle?
Pick up HER COWBOY HERO to find out.
Available January 2015, wherever
Love Inspired® books and ebooks are sold.